BILL HILL'S PILLS

BOOK 2 IN THE TWINKLE TEXAS COZY MYSTERY SERIES

DAWN GREENFIELD IRELAND

ARTISTIC
ORIGINS

CONTENTS

Acknowledgments   vii
Also by Dawn Greenfield Ireland   ix
Map of Twinkle & Human Characters   xi

Chapter 1   1
Chapter 2   10
Chapter 3   20
Chapter 4   30
Chapter 5   39
Chapter 6   48
Chapter 7   58
Chapter 8   67
Chapter 9   77
Chapter 10   87
Chapter 11   97
Chapter 12   107
Chapter 13   117
Chapter 14   127
Chapter 15   136
Chapter 16   144
Chapter 17   154
Chapter 18   164
Chapter 19   175
Chapter 20   186
Chapter 21   195

More Twinkle! Book 3   199
About the Author   201

Bill Hill's Pills by Dawn Greenfield Ireland

Published by Artistic Origins

Copyright © 2021 Dawn Greenfield Ireland

Corrections 2/14/2024, 2/20/2026, 4/29/2026

Cover image: Brandon White VictoryLaurel.com 5/2026

Map of Twinkle, Texas created by @agus_kupit on Fiverr.com Added 3/31/2024

Interior layout by Yours Truly (me)

ISBN 9781940385464 (eBook)

ISBN 9781940385471 (paperback)

Dawn Greenfield Ireland Artistic Origins Inc.

https://www.degreenfield.com

Publisher's Note: This is a work of fiction. Names, characters, places, and incidents are a product of the author's imagination. Locales and public names are sometimes used for atmospheric purposes. Any resemblance to actual people, living or dead, or to businesses, companies, events, institutions, or locales is completely coincidental.

This book may contain references to specific commercial products, process or service by trade name, trademark, manufacturer, or otherwise, specific brand-name products and/or trade names of products, which are trademarks or registered trademarks and/or trade names, and these are property of their respective owners.

Dawn Greenfield Ireland or her associates, have no association with any specific commercial products, process, or service by trade name, trademark, manufacturer, or otherwise, specific brand-name products and/or trade names of products.

Please purchase only authorized electronic editions, and do not participate in or encourage electronic piracy of copyrighted materials. Your support of the author's rights is appreciated.

Please visit my website: http://www.degreenfield.com/ and sign up for my newsletter and get the latest news before the public.

Be kind = Leave a review where you bought/downloaded the book.

HINT: don't regurgitate the synopsis for your review. Just tell people what you liked, didn't like – that's what people want – your opinion.

 Formatted with Vellum

ACKNOWLEDGMENTS

How do books get completed? By a team of helpful people!

Many thanks to Monica and Curtis Hightower for help with a couple of medical situations that required information about how things would be done in a real-life situation.

Once again, my pal Joe Thompson helped me with the legal wording in the chapters. I'm forever grateful for all your help. Thanks for putting up with my craziness in all these scenarios!

Brandon White VictoryLaurel.com, my eldest son created the new cover 5/2026.

You know I'm forever grateful for my editing team and readers: Jeff Gonyea, Cicely Wynne, Dickie Stone, and Monica Hightower. I can still feel the sting of the ruler across my knuckles!

Many thanks to @agus_kupit on Fiverr.com for the incredible map of Twinkle, Texas!

Actions Appreciated

Please leave a review on the retailer website where you purchased the book, or on my website! Reviews help authors get recognized, get the word out, and sell more books. I will love you forever if you leave a review!

HINT: Don't regurgitate the synopsis for your review. Just tell people what you liked, didn't like. That's what people want... your opinion.

Every word I have written and published is from my noggin (brain, in case you don't know what noggin means). My fiction is all make-believe, from the deep dive into my wild imagination. All my nonfiction books have been researched until my brain has scrambled.

Nonfiction	
The Puppy Baby Book	Mastering Your Money (2022)
Puppy Adoption and Beyond	Writers Preparation Handbook
Mastering Your Money (2008)	What's Breaking Your Budget
Online Classes	
Writers Preparation Handbook	How to Format Word Docs Like A Pro
Cozy Mysteries	**Sci-Fi-Fantasy**
The Alcott Family Adventures	**The Thol Series**
Hot Chocolate	Prophecy of Thol
Bitter Chocolate	Gifts From Thol
Spicy Chocolate	Love of Thol
Nutty Chocolate	King of Thol
Katz' Cat Series	Earth Calling Thol
Katz' Cat	**Sci-Fi Romance Adventure**
Bill Hill's Pills	Forced Dreams
The Detectives	**Dystopian**
Coming in 2025: The Pact	The Last Dog
	Texmexzona
Books by my Alter Ego ~ DG Ireland	
Bonded Shapeshifter Billionaire Series	
Bonded	
Tothars	
Tilted	
Unforeseen	
Connected	
Need A Notebook?	
See my 54 themed notebooks on my website **www.degreenfield.com/notebooks**	
Screenplays formatted as books	
Plan B (Dark Comedy)	Where's Ralphie? (Family Comedy)
The God Child (Action Adventure)	Standing Dead (Drama/Tragedy)
The Far Corner (Sci-Fi/Psychological/Creatures)	
Screenplays as TV Episodes	
Hot Chocolate ~ Episode 1	Prophecy of Thol ~ Episode 1
Bonded ~ Episode 1	
See my screenplays on my website: degreenfield.com **Filmfreeway, CoverFly, ISA Network**	

Map of Twinkle

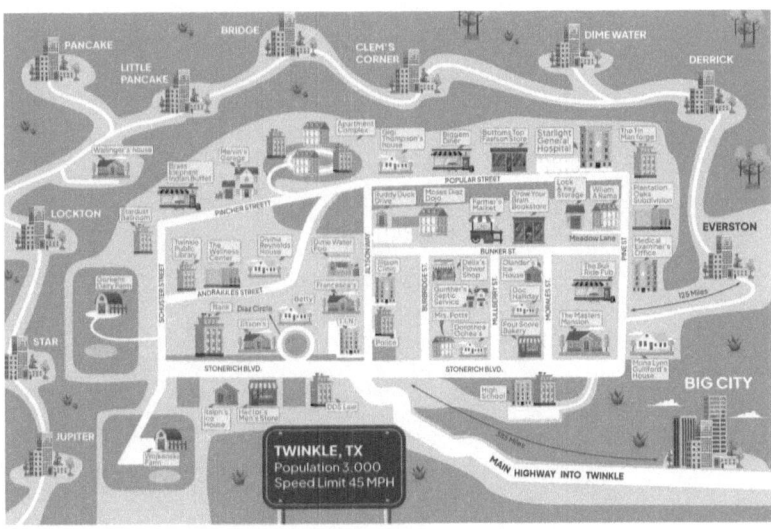

The Human Characters

Jimmy Katz, the main character in the Katz' Cat / Twinkle, TX cozy mystery book series

Mrs. Potts, the boardinghouse landlady in the Katz' Cat / Twinkle, TX cozy mystery book series

Chief Price in the Katz' Cat / Twinkle, TX cozy mystery book series

Brian, Jimmy's best friend from the Big City who moves to Twinkle in the Katz' Cat / Twinkle, TX cozy mystery

CHAPTER ONE

"Where's breakfast?" Guppy squawked in his bellowing voice. The Amazon parrot clung to the footboard, digging his talons into the queen bed while Maddy, his kitty partner in crime, took more aggressive action.

Jimmy Katz jerked out of a deep sleep as a champagne-colored paw with tabby stripes patted his face. Then the kitten yanked his sandy-colored hair into her mouth.

One droopy baby blue eye popped open. Jimmy caught his kitten Maddy grabbing a mouthful of his hair, getting ready to yank again.

"Maddy? Did Guppy put you up to this? Why can't daddy sleep until the alarm goes off?" Jimmy croaked out with what he thought was early morning dry throat.

The alarm clock screamed.

Jimmy flung his hand to slam down the stop button, missed, and accidentally whacked his windup clock off the nightstand.

The alarm clanged through his brain.

He lurched off the bed to grab the offending clock and tumbled onto the floor.

"So, this is the way it's going to be today?" Jimmy rasped. He grabbed the clock, silenced the alarm, and returned it to the nightstand. As he pulled himself off the floor to stand, the room spun. He plunked his butt onto the bed and wiped his hands down his face. "That can't be good."

He gave it another try and made it to his feet without spinning. Goosebumps pebbled his arms. He walked across the bedroom floor and grabbed his robe off the hook on the back of the door. Then he slipped his feet into his house shoes.

"Come on, everybody. Let's get breakfast," he grumbled.

Guppy flew past him to his fake tree in the living room. He settled onto the sturdy branch and glanced at his empty food bowl. "Where's breakfast?"

Jimmy stumbled into the living room, grabbed the empty food bowl and the stainless water bowl out of the stand attached to Guppy's tree.

"Coming right up, your majesty," Jimmy mumbled. He returned to the kitchen, dodging Maddy. "Will you two please give me a moment?"

He dumped the water into the sink and scrubbed the water bowl, filled it and returned to the tree. "Fresh water. Food's on its way."

Jimmy flipped the switch on the prepared coffee maker. He opened the refrigerator and retrieved Guppy's food bins and Maddy's canned wet food. Once he fed his animals, he scrambled four eggs, made two pieces of toast, and poured his coffee. He flopped into a chair at the table and slowly ate his meal and drank his coffee.

He sat there like a dullard and silently assessed himself. His right ear hurt. Jimmy swallowed and discovered his throat was sore. He dragged himself into the bathroom, showered then dressed. Jimmy opened the apartment door and forced one foot in front of the other down the stairs. Brian's door was open, so his friend was most likely at work at the newspaper office. He headed to the kitchen to get Mrs. Potts' expert advice.

He found his plump landlady at the table reading the morning paper. "Morning, Mrs. Potts."

Her head of shocking white, spiky hair with purple streaks jerked up. "Sounds like you're coming down with something, Jimmy. Go to the Wellness Center. Bill Hill will fix you up."

"The Wellness Center? Where's it located?" Jimmy asked.

"Over by the library. You can't miss the blue door," Mrs. Potts said.

"Okay. I'll be back soon. Think I may go back to bed," Jimmy said. He headed down the hallway to the front door.

JIMMY SPOTTED the store with the blue door and pulled into a parking place. He dragged himself out of the car and opened the door of the shop. A bell tinkled as he entered. He approached the counter where a middle-aged man stood decked out in a T-shirt with a huge pink heart on the front, and worn jeans. Several necklaces sporting peace signs, and quartz crystals hung around his neck. Stud earrings that looked like they might be diamonds adorned his ears.

"May I help you?" the man asked.

"Are you Bill Hill?" Jimmy croaked out. He was getting worse by the minute.

"That's me. You don't sound too good. What hurts?" Bill asked.

"Ear and throat," Jimmy said.

Bill Hill came around the counter in his Birkenstock sandals. He pointed a digital thermometer at Jimmy's forehead. A beep sounded. "You're running a temperature. Let me get something to help you." He took off among the shelves and returned to the counter with three items. One hand tapped a large bottle. "Wellness In A Bottle, my own formula. Take six capsules twice a day until you feel better."

He tapped a bottle that contained a dropper. "Colloidal Silver. Fill a glass with no less than two ounces of water, then add three squeezes to the water and drink it once a day."

He tapped a box of Gypsy Cold Care tea by Traditional Medicinals. "This is an excellent tea for when you don't feel well, and especially if you feel chilled. Steep one bag in water for 10-15 minutes before drinking. Add honey. These three things are my doctor prevention remedy I've been using for the past twenty-five years."

Bill rang up the sale. "Go to bed after you dose yourself."

"Thanks, Bill." Jimmy dragged himself out to the car and drove back to Mrs. Potts' boarding house. He climbed the steps, unlocked the front door, and trudged down the hall into the kitchen where he found his landlady at the stove making chicken soup while Maddy the cat supervised.

Guppy was perched on his favorite chair back as he watched squirrels leap from limb to limb in the mighty oak trees in the backyard, beyond the gazebo. "Invaders!" he squawked.

Jimmy cringed at the loud bird.

"I'm going back to bed after I take this stuff," Jimmy said as he shook the bag. He turned to his bird. "Keep it down, Guppy. Those squirrels will not get into the house."

"Are you running a fever?" Mrs. Potts asked.

"Yeah. I'll make this tea after I take a nap," Jimmy said. He turned and slogged down the hall and up the stairs.

TWO HOURS LATER, Jimmy sat at the kitchen table in his apartment with a cup of tea in front of him. A tap sounded on his door.

"Come in," he hollered out in a rough voice.

"Call the cops! Guppy belted out.

Danny Stonerich, Jimmy's coworker at the Twinkle Independent News, along with his friend Brian McKinley who had transplanted himself in Twinkle from The Big City, came inside and wandered over to the table.

"Knock it off, Guppy," Brian said.

"Man, you sound awful." Danny pulled out his phone and snapped a picture.

"Did you go to the doctor?" Brian asked.

"Went to Bill Hill's place and got some stuff," Jimmy said.

"What kind of place is that?" Brian asked.

"It's the Wellness Center," Danny said. When he saw Brian's scrunched eyebrows, he spelled it out. "Vitamin store with a lot of different stuff to stay healthy."

"Oh!" Brian got it.

"What's going on at the TIN?" Jimmy asked.

"We were going to ask you to come to the Biggem Diner to catch the local flavor," Danny said. "But it doesn't look like a good idea."

"I'm going back to bed after I drink this tea," Jimmy said.

The doorbell rang.

Guppy squawked "Invaders!" as he flew out of the apartment and landed on the bannister near the front door.

"Guppy, go to the kitchen," Mrs. Potts commanded.

They heard the bird squawk as he flew away.

Mrs. Potts opened the front door and talked to someone. Then two distinct pairs of shoes climbed the stairs. Betty Diaz entered the apartment with Toombs, her trusted employee. Toombs deposited a sack onto the table.

"Jimmy, you look terrible. Why aren't you in bed?" Jimmy's great-aunt Betty asked.

"Tea..." He held up the cup.

Toombs opened the sack and deposited Vick's VapoRub, a bottle of ibuprofen, and a digital thermometer onto the table. He removed the thermometer from the packaging. Betty rescued the instructions Toombs tossed into the trash.

"If you're not better by Wednesday, Dr. Canada (pronounced Kah-nah-dah) will make a house call." Betty drilled her eyes into her great-nephew. No one stood a chance when she cast her firm pronouncements.

As the recently discovered heir of the Katz-Diaz fortune who almost didn't survive a murderous head librarian, Jimmy couldn't walk down the street without being scrutinized by the population of Twinkle, Texas, the county seat of Starlight County. They all felt it was their responsibility to protect the heir.

His great-aunt might be ninety, but Betty Katz-Diaz was no simpering weakling. As the head of the huge dynasty, she was grooming Jimmy to take over the family business worth billions with an S.

Betty walked out of the apartment to the top of the stairs. "Bertha? Are you down there?"

Mrs. Potts hurried to the bottom of the stairs and looked up.

"Bertha, set your phone calendar to call Dr. Canada on Wednesday if Jimmy isn't better," Betty said.

"I'm making chicken soup. He'll be okay soon. He needs bed rest right now," Mrs. Potts hinted.

Betty nodded, turned, and marched back into the apartment. "Everyone out. Let Jimmy get back to bed."

Danny and Brian hurried past the town matriarch before they were verbally lashed. Toombs waited for his boss at the top of the stairs.

Ever since Betty had taken flight on the stairs at the mansion from a rigged stair by a crazy librarian's plot, Toombs not only packed his gun in a shoulder holster, but he made sure he preceded her going downstairs in case she tripped... or was pushed, so he could break her fall. Even though those dark days were behind them, if one resident of Twinkle could hatch such a diabolical plan, he wasn't taking any chances.

OFFICER CELEBRITY MASTERS waved to Danny and Brian as Danny's car pulled away from the curb. She slipped into their parking place behind the familiar black Lincoln Town Car that Toombs escorted Twinkle's matriarch around town in. She shifted the car into park, drew her fingers through her long, wavy blonde hair, and checked her teeth for spinach in the flip-down mirror on the visor. Satisfied, she opened the door and climbed out of the cop car.

The tan shirt and brown pants of the police department uniform sinfully hugged her curves. Celebrity snuck a look in several directions, then unbuttoned the top two buttons. She considered the third button, but decided against it. She didn't want Mrs. Diaz or Mrs. Potts to change their opinion of her.

Celebrity climbed the steps and rapped on the door.

After a couple of minutes, Mrs. Potts opened the door. "Well, hello, Celebrity. Going to play nurse today?"

The police officer scrunched her forehead. "Nurse?"

"Jimmy's sick," Mrs. Potts offered up. "Bill Hill provided help, and Mrs. Diaz brought more supplies."

"Oh, no. Is it the flu?" Celebrity asked.

"It's either the flu or an allergy," Mrs. Potts said. "Betty gave him until Wednesday to get better, then I have to call Dr. Canada."

"Let me go see for myself," Celebrity said, as she rushed up the stairs and slammed into a hard wall, otherwise known as Toombs.

"Oof! Oh, I'm so sorry, Toombs," she stammered.

Toombs reached out and grabbed Celebrity's shoulder before she bounced off him and crashed down the stairs. "Everything's fine."

"How's Jimmy?" she asked.

"Looks like he was steamrolled," Toombs said.

Celebrity went inside the apartment and greeted Betty. "Hi, Mrs. Diaz. Where's Jimmy?"

"Hello Celebrity. He just went back to bed," Betty said. "I'll leave you to visit him while Toombs escorts me over to the DDS office."

The first time anyone new to town heard *DDS*, they automatically thought of a dentist's office. Pete Daigle, Judson Diaz and Godfrey (Stoney) Stonerich were the DDS law firm partners. Junior Stonerich hadn't made partner yet and typically filled the capacity of court-appointed attorney when the need arose.

DDS served the Katz-Diaz conglomerate headed by Betty Diaz. She spent her days and evenings Zooming with corporate staff about the many projects that spanned across the globe and comprised billions of dollars' worth of investments and charities.

Celebrity headed back to the bedroom where she found Jimmy huddled under a big comforter. "Hi Jimmy. Oh, wow, you look terrible."

The sick man opened his eyes and offered up a weak smile to the angel before him. "Hi Celebrity. Don't get too close." He coughed.

"You're in terrible shape. You sure you don't want Dr.

Canada to come over today?" Celebrity thought he needed the doctor sooner than Wednesday.

"I'm good. Bill Hill fixed me up with a bunch of stuff, then Aunt Betty brought more stuff," Jimmy said.

"Try to get some sleep. Bed rest is very important when you're not feeling well." Celebrity bit her bottom lip. She pulled the comforter up around his shoulders so his neck wouldn't be exposed to the breeze from the ceiling fan. "I'll come back later when I'm finished with my shift."

"K."

She quietly left the bedroom and returned to the living room. Maddy was napping on her pillow, but Guppy wasn't around. She hunkered down and ran her hand down Maddy's head to her tail. "Hello, little girl. Your daddy doesn't feel good, so you and Guppy are in charge, okay?"

Maddy meowed as if she understood Celebrity.

Celebrity left the apartment door open to allow Maddy the freedom to go downstairs. She trudged down the stairs and turned toward the kitchen, where the parrot was busy catching shelled peas Mrs. Potts rolled across the table to keep him entertained and somewhat quiet.

"How did he get so sick overnight?" Celebrity asked.

"Maybe he slept with the window open," Mrs. Potts said.

"I'll be back later when I get off work," Celebrity said.

CHAPTER TWO

CELEBRITY RE-BUTTONED her shirt once she was in her police car before taking off to the station. Halfway there, she spotted Caleb Armbruster staggering down the street. The town drunk typically wasn't wandering around at this time of day, so she slowed to watch what he was up to. Just as he reached down and picked up a rock, Celebrity hit her siren, making it send out a loud twerp. She flashed the top lights as well then steered the cruiser to the side of the road and got out.

"Caleb, you weren't about to throw that rock through the store window, were you?"

The drunk swayed on the sidewalk. "Who are you?" He hadn't dropped the rock.

"Officer Masters. Twinkle police. You don't remember me?"

"Never seen you before," Caleb said.

"Drop the rock, Caleb."

"Whatcha going to do ifen I don't?" He hauled off and threw the rock at her.

Celebrity threw up her arms to protect herself, but the rock bounced off her right temple. She collapsed to the ground, out cold.

The stunned drunk staggered back a couple of steps. He eyed the open driver's door on the police car, hurled himself toward it and got inside. Caleb slammed the door shut and drove away.

DETECTIVE BENITO RAMIREZ drove down Main Street on his way back to the police station. He swigged coffee and returned it to his cup holder. He dragged his hand through his dark brown hair to get it out of his eyes, disappointed that the new hair product didn't tame his thick mane. Ramirez spotted something up ahead on the road. As he rolled closer, he recognized the shape of a body in what he thought was a police uniform. He turned on his police lights, rushed out of the car and discovered Celebrity.

He was on his radio in a heartbeat. "Send an ambulance to Delia's flower shop immediately!" He disconnected, then called Chief Kenton Price.

"Chief! Someone attacked Celebrity! I called an ambulance. She's out cold! Her car's not here!"

The wail of the ambulance approached fast. The driver pulled to the curb, doors flew open, and they grabbed equipment. Two attendants rushed to the fallen police officer as a cop car screeched to a stop and the chief rushed to the sidewalk, staying out of the way of the EMTs, but hovering to look over his deputy.

"What happened?" Chief Price bellowed.

Ramirez shook his head. "Don't know. This was how I found her."

The EMTs loaded Celebrity onto a gurney, hauled her to the rear of the ambulance and took off to the hospital.

Chief Price called dispatch. "Stephanie, put an APB out on Celebrity's car! It's got to be around here somewhere." He disconnected. "Ramirez, get ahold of FeBe Morales and see if there's a camera at that ATM over there. Maybe we can get footage of what happened here."

The chief looked around and noticed the rock on the road. "Looks like that rock could have been used as a weapon." He walked to his car, popped open the trunk, dug into a case and extracted an evidence bag and a glove. He returned to the rock, took a couple of pictures to capture the location, then slipped the glove on and bagged the rock as evidence.

"See what you can dig up, Ramirez. Are any of these stores open? Get Peterson and Dupont over here to canvas these shop owners. I'm heading to the hospital," Chief Price barked out.

Practically the entire newspaper staff arrived at the same time as the two cops.

"What happened?" asked Sylvan Stonerich, Twinkle Independent News (TIN) publisher. "We heard on the scanner that Celebrity was attacked!"

Bill Trance, the managing editor, nodded to the stone in the evidence bag. "That the weapon?"

"We don't really know anything, just speculation," Price said as he raised the evidence bag.

"Any suspects?" Danny asked.

The chief shook his head. "Hopefully, someone saw something." He got into his car, enabled the siren and lights, and rushed away toward the hospital. Less than seven minutes later, he parked and entered the hospital. He stopped at the emergency room information desk.

"What's the status of my deputy?"

"Let me call Dr. Canada," the woman said.

After a lengthy wait, Dr. Canada approached the police chief. Price noticed the doctor's tight face. He steeled himself for bad news.

"Kenton, she hasn't come around yet. Luckily, her skull didn't fracture when her head hit the pavement. Celebrity has a severe concussion. We performed a CT scan of her head and neck, and thankfully it revealed only minor cerebral bruising and swelling. But since the trauma was significant enough to leave her unconscious, we've admitted her for observation and moved her from the ER to a room upstairs," Dr. Canada said.

"Irving, level with me. Is Celebrity going to make it?" Chief Price masked his fear. He couldn't believe anyone would want to hurt sweet Celebrity.

Dr. Canada steered Chief Price away from the information desk by the elbow. "It's a waiting game at this point. We have to wait for her to wake up. If the fluid or swelling in her skull increases significantly, we may need to do a procedure to reduce intracranial pressure."

Brian trotted over to the chief and the doctor. "What can you tell me that we can print?"

THE NEXT MORNING, Mrs. Potts sat at the kitchen table drinking her morning coffee and eating a homemade honey bun as she unfolded the newspaper.

DEPUTY ATTACKED ON MAIN STREET

"Oh, my goodness!" She forgot all about her coffee and pastry and delved into the article. "Not Celebrity!" She grabbed the paper, jumped to her feet, and clambered up the stairs. "Jimmy!"

She reached the top of the stairs and rapped on her tenant's door. After a long moment, she opened the door and stormed inside. "Jimmy? Jimmy, where are you?"

Jimmy tied his robe as he walked into the kitchen. "What's going on?"

He looked and sounded much better. Mrs. Potts held the newspaper open for him to see the headline.

"Someone attacked Celebrity yesterday after she left here!" Mrs. Potts wailed. "I wondered why she didn't come back here after her work shift."

Jimmy snatched the newspaper from Mrs. Potts, noticed that Danny wrote the article, and grabbed his cellphone. "Danny, what happened?" He listened to his friend and coworker. He nodded, then shook his head. "Okay. Thanks." He disconnected the call and got Chief Price on the phone. "What do you know about Celebrity's attacker so far?" His face glowed with fury. "Mrs. Potts, I'm going to the hospital!"

"But you're sick!"

"I feel better. It's obviously not something contagious like the flu."

"Ah, hon, you'd better get dressed first," his landlady suggested.

Jimmy looked down and realized he was barefoot and wearing his robe. "Good idea." He turned and rushed to his bedroom. In less than fifteen minutes, he showered, shampooed, shaved, and wore his good clothes, including a jacket that concealed his shoulder holster. Ever since the earlier break-ins and attempted murder events, Chief Price threatened bodily harm if Jimmy ever left the boarding house without his weapon.

He stormed into the hospital and approached the front desk. "What room is Celebrity Masters in?"

The man at the desk recognized Jimmy and checked the patient roster on the computer. "204."

Jimmy nodded, then took off toward the stairs. He climbed them two at a time and yanked the door open on the second floor. He studied the number scheme on the wall plaque and turned to his right. Jimmy found 204 and went inside.

Celebrity was sleeping. Her head was bandaged. There was an IV in her arm, and she was hooked up to heart and vital monitors. Jimmy walked over to the bed and sank into the visitor chair. He picked up her hand and set it into his, running his thumb over the top of her hand.

"Come on, Celebrity. Don't be in a coma."

She was so still. It didn't look natural, and Jimmy thought dark thoughts. He distracted himself by looking around the room. There were several plants, vases, and flower pots. He pulled his phone out and made a call. He whispered into the phone. "Mrs. Potts, can you send flowers to the hospital? Something really beautiful, no matter the cost. I don't care if they have to import them! Room 204. Thanks."

A few minutes later, Chief Price came into the room. "Has she woken up yet?"

Jimmy shook his head. "She hasn't even twitched. I'm really worried, chief."

"We arrested Armbruster. Looks like he'll finally dry out because he's going away for quite a long time," the chief said. "Wrecked the cruiser. Feel bad for his family, but this was a long time coming."

"Did he tell you what happened?" Jimmy asked.

"Had no idea he did anything wrong. If it hadn't been for the camera at the ATM, we wouldn't have a suspect. He abandoned the car, but his prints are all over the steering wheel, gearshift, and other places that could only be accessed from the driver's seat, so it's not like he can weasel out of the charges for stealing and wrecking it." Chief Price shook his head, sad and angry at the same time. "Pretty sure no one will bail him out."

A nurse entered the room carrying a digital tablet. "Hello. I'm nurse Jeanetta and I'll only be a minute." She took readings from the bedside vital monitor and noted how much saline was left in the IV bag. She typed her visual readings into the tablet.

"Would you mind stepping back so I can close the curtain?"

Jimmy reluctantly stood. He and the chief left the room.

The nurse noted the amount of urine in the catheter bag, shut off the flow into the bag, and emptied the contents into the toilet. She replaced the bag, opened the flow valve, then ran a washcloth under warm water, wrung it out and slowly swiped it across Celebrity's face. She applied a lip balm so the deputy's lips would not become chapped—everyone knew and liked Celebrity Masters, and a little lip balm would keep those plump lips soft.

When she finished her ministrations, the nurse opened the curtain and left the room to attend to another patient.

JIMMY HEADED over to the mansion. It had been a few days since he had visited his great aunt and discussed business. He was learning all aspects of the vast Katz-Diaz projects, investments, and charities, and had attended Zoom meetings. Betty introduced him as her heir to managers, CEOs, executives and the like—anyone involved with the Katz-Diaz holdings.

Jenkins opened the door. "Hello, Jimmy. Your great-aunt will be delighted to see you up and about."

"Have you heard about Celebrity?" Jimmy asked.

"We just found out about it this morning," the butler said. "Is there any more news?"

"The chief arrested the town drunk. Celebrity seems to be in a coma, though," Jimmy said. "It's a waiting game."

Jenkins patted Jimmy's shoulder. "It will work out the way it's supposed to."

Jimmy's shoulders slumped. "Yeah." He left the doorway and headed back to his aunt's office. He tapped on the open doorframe. "Hi Aunt Betty."

She recognized his flat tone. "It's a shame about Celebrity, but don't give up on her. She'll pull through."

Jimmy slipped into a chair in front of the vast desk. "I know, but when? She hasn't even twitched."

"Look on the bright side. There's no internal bleeding. Dr. Canada said the scans showed nothing too serious. That's a blessing. The rest is up to her." Betty looked her great-nephew over. "You certainly revived overnight."

"Between Mrs. Potts' chicken soup and Bill Hill's pills and stuff, whatever was trying to latch onto me flew the coop," Jimmy said.

"What's on your schedule today?" Betty already knew, but figured she would try to distract Jimmy from his sadness over Celebrity.

"Toombs and I are going to the shooting range to practice. Then Moses is going to beat me to the floor at the dojo. He calls it self-protection training, but I think it's payback for something. Then I'll head over to DDS for mind-numbing explanations of legal terms regarding the contracts and stuff," Jimmy recited.

"Good. It's best to stay busy," his aunt said. "Now shoo. I've got a Zoom meeting in two minutes."

JIMMY LEFT the mansion and trudged across the vast lawn to the practice area that Toombs had set up. His mentor was waiting under the umbrella his aunt insisted upon setting up for them to find relief from the blazing Texas sun in-between shooting sets.

"You sure look better today," Toombs said as he looked over at his student.

"I really felt terrible yesterday," Jimmy admitted. "Chicken soup and Bill Hill's Wellness In A Bottle did the trick." He pulled his gun out of his shoulder holster and handed it over to Toombs.

His mentor looked over the Heckler and Koch VP9 with a 9-round magazine. When he was satisfied that Jimmy kept up the cleaning and maintenance of his weapon, he handed it back.

"You packing a spare clip?" Toombs asked.

Jimmy patted the inside pocket of his jacket. Toombs nodded.

A young man walked across the lawn carrying a shotgun and a rifle. When he arrived at the umbrella, he placed the weapons across the table.

"Jimmy, this is Klive. He'll be our running boy," Toombs said.

Jimmy and Klive shook hands.

"Ready?" Toombs asked.

Jimmy's first round was off.

"Listen, you can't let emotions get between you and a threat. You have to always be on top of your game, otherwise you could end up shot, or dead." Toombs glared at his student. "Now, show me what you've got."

Jimmy pulled himself together and focused on the target. He let his finger pull the trigger while his eyes never left the bullseye.

"That's more like it. You Katz' sure can hit the target. Your aunt blows out the bullseye every time without fail. Let's move on to the rifle, then the shotgun."

An hour and a quarter later, Jimmy was on his back with Moses Diaz grinning wickedly down at him. "Come on, Jimmy. Get in the game."

CHAPTER THREE

By THREE THAT AFTERNOON, Jimmy had fled the offices of DDS. Corporate charts, graphs, lists, and the whole Corporate Social Responsibility (CSR) policies and practices flooded his head. He didn't think he would ever fully grasp all that DDS and his great-aunt took for granted and thought he would easily absorb.

He headed over to the Bull Ride and approached Annie at the hostess stand. Jimmy was relieved that Annie had gotten over her quest to haul him down the aisle and had settled into a friendly acquaintance instead.

"Hey, Jimmy. Everything okay? You look like you stared into the headlights too long," she quipped.

"Just left DDS. I'm surprised I can recognize my name," he joked.

"Well, come on. Horace will take care of you," Annie said, as she led him over to Horace's section of tables and seated him. "Want a beer?"

"No, I think I'll stick with iced tea. Have to go to the hospital and check on Celebrity later," he said.

Annie rushed back to the hostess stand to greet customers.

Horace approached his favorite customer. They fist-bumped. "Hey, man. We're introducing a meaty veggie burger. Interested?"

Jimmy grimaced and shot Horace an *Are you serious* look. "I'll eat one right after I see you chow down first."

"Looks like you dodged that bullet. My sister was a vegan for over fifteen years, but her Big City doctor said she wasn't getting enough protein, so now she's eating chicken and seafood. I doubt she'll ever join me for a steak dinner, though." Horace nodded knowingly. "What can I get you today?"

A server slipped in and set a tall glass of iced tea in front of Jimmy.

"Thanks," he said. Jimmy always thanked the wait staff. It wasn't too long ago when he was a working stiff in The Big City with not great wages. His old boss never cared one whit whether he was making enough to pay his bills. All he had been interested in was filling column inches for the readers.

Jimmy knew the menu by heart, but had to figure out what he was hungry for, so he glanced over the plastic-coated offerings. It was between lunch and dinner, and he knew Mrs. Potts would have something good waiting for him when he came home. "Let me have the double club with a side of fruit." He handed the menu back to Horace when he was joined by Brian and Danny.

His friends didn't ask whether they could join him; they just grabbed chairs and sat.

"Whatcha having?" Danny asked. He grabbed the menu from Horace. He and Brian looked it over.

"Double club," Jimmy said. He nudged Brian. "Don't forget supper time."

"Yeah, I'll have the same," Brian said.

"Make it three," Danny said.

"You want fruit or fries on the side?" Horace asked.

Danny ordered the fries, and Brian opted for the fruit so he wouldn't be too full to do justice to Mrs. Potts' food. No one ever wanted to turn down her cooking.

"What's new?" Jimmy asked.

"Rimpole Diggelosky's new cookbook hit the Amazon best-seller list. He's going to do a book signing Thursday," Danny said.

"I heard he's going to tour all the Texas big cities," Brian said.

"No kidding? Wow! Good for him. Where's he going to be Thursday?" Jimmy asked.

"Dime Water Foo(d)," Danny said. "He's going to give a plug for Wojkenski's vegetables when he tours."

JIMMY STOOD in line to get two copies of Rimpole's new cookbook. He was surprised at the turnout, but figured people from Clems Corner, Jupiter, Lockton, Pancake, Derrick, Dime Water, Bridge and Star had come out in droves. He finally paid for his books and stood before the big guy.

"Hey, Jimmy. Thanks for coming out to support me. Who do you want the book to be autographed for?" Rimpole asked.

"Sign one for Mrs. Potts, and the other one for Celebrity," Jimmy said.

"How's Celebrity doing?" the cook asked.

"Still in a coma," Jimmy said.

Rimpole grabbed a book, opened the cover and wrote out a personal autograph:

To Mrs. Potts. Thank you for teaching me how to cook!
Rim

He grabbed another book and signed his standard autograph:

Eat healthy.
Rimpole Diggelosky

His signature was a scrawl. The R, D and Y were the only recognizable letters.

"Thanks, Rim. Congratulations on the Amazon bestseller list. I'll see you later." Jimmy stepped away from the table and spotted Mrs. Potts in line. He walked her way and handed her the book.

"You bought me a book? I was going to have him autograph it for me," she said. Then she opened the cover and saw his note. "Oh, that sweet man! Thank you, Jimmy. I will cherish this book forever... after I see how he's changed since I taught him in school."

"It's good to see someone local have success," he said. "I'm going to head over to the hospital. I bought a book for Celebrity. She'd have been here to support Rim."

They parted ways in the parking lot, and Jimmy headed over to the hospital. He and Chief Price arrived outside the front doors at the same time, so Jimmy rode the elevator up to the second floor with the chief.

"Were there a lot of people at the book signing?" the chief asked.

"Yeah. I was surprised so many came out for a cookbook," Jimmy said.

They entered the hospital room. It didn't look like anything had changed. Jimmy took a chair by the bed, and the chief settled into the other one beside him. They talked in hushed tones about goings-on around town. One minute later, Celebrity opened her eyes and blinked.

"Hey, Celebrity. You ready to get out of that bed and get back to work?" Chief Price asked.

She looked from the chief to Jimmy. "Work? Motherhood's a full-time job, chief. I won't be going back to work until the kids start school." She settled her eyes on Jimmy. "Who's watching the kids, Jimmy?" She flung the covers back and swung her feet over the edge of the bed, and was yanked back by the attached catheter and other equipment sensors.

"Kids? I never knew you had kids, Celebrity." Jimmy was floored.

The chief stood. "Be right back." He hurried out of the room.

"It can't be that bad!" Celebrity huffed at Jimmy.

The Katz-Diaz heir stared at the woman he had been wanting to ask out on a date. "We don't have any kids, and we're not married."

Chief Price returned with Dr. Canada in tow.

"Hello, Celebrity," Dr. Canada said. "Glad to see you're back with us."

Her forehead crunched. "Why am I in the hospital?"

"You attempted to apprehend Caleb Armbruster, but he hit you in the head with a rock," Chief Price said.

"Surely you're mistaken. I haven't worked for the police department since Tulip was born," Celebrity stated. "She's four and Dorchester is two."

"Tulip? I'd never agree to give any of my kids a farm animal name," Jimmy stated firmly. "Dorchester? These kids would be tormented their entire lives with those hair-brained names."

The chief laid a hand on Jimmy's shoulder to calm him. There was something weirdly wrong. He glanced over at Doc Canada. "Any clue?"

"Why don't I schedule tests? Looks like a whole new reality has come forward," Dr. Canada said.

Jimmy left the hospital and went to the boarding house. He slipped into a chair in Mrs. Potts' kitchen, looking like someone had knocked him through a loop.

"What's wrong?" his landlady asked. "Did something happen at the hospital?"

"You could say that. Celebrity seems to think we're married with two kids. Tulip and Dorchester. Where she ever got those names, I have no idea." Jimmy's head spun from the conversation. "Dr. Canada's going to run tests."

"Oh, no," Mrs. Potts said.

"What if she doesn't snap out of this? I've never even asked her out on a date!"

"Maybe this is her projecting what she wants in her future, Jimmy. I know it's strange, especially those names, but if that's her reality right now, everyone will have to play along," Mrs. Potts said.

THE CHIEF and Doc Canada had their hands full. Celebrity was worried about her phantom children. Who was going to feed and take care of them? Chief Price finally convinced her that Jimmy left to go do those things. Doc Canada called in a colleague who specialized in psychological problems associated with patients coming out of a coma, which is called post-traumatic amnesia (PTA).

Dr. Moore explained how false memories worked. Celebrity's mind didn't have any day-to-day memories when she was in the coma. Her brain was trying to fill in the gap of that time and found memories that may have been associated with books she read, conversations she had in the past, TV shows or movies she had watched.

All they could do was wait for fresh memories to form. Dr.

Moore explained that PTA sometimes lasted three to four times longer than the actual coma. Patients' emotions could range from disbelief in the current situation to combative—fighting to be released from the tubes connecting them to machines, and everything in between.

When they sat Jimmy down to explain the problem, he could hardly believe what he heard. "Do we all pretend and go along with this make-believe life? What about her parents? What about her job?"

"Well, Celebrity has her own apartment. Her folks live up near Dallas," the chief said.

"How are we going to manifest these two kids?" Jimmy asked, on the edge of panic. "I've never taken care of little kids!"

The next three weeks were a nightmare. Jimmy hired two guards to stand outside the hospital room door in shifts, so Celebrity didn't take off to parts unknown. The nurses, guards and visitors were schooled to follow along with the story Celebrity had in her head. Then, on Tuesday, she woke and remembered who she was and what her life involved.

She picked up the hospital phone on the nightstand and called work. "Hey, do I have to wait before I come back to work when I get discharged?"

Chief Price practically fell out of his chair. "Let me check our insurance policy. You might need to get a release from the doctor. He might want you to rest up for a few days or a week after you're discharged."

"I can't wait to get out of here. Did you arrest Caleb?"

"Caleb isn't going anywhere for a long time. He wrecked your cruiser, so you'll have to be on desk duty, or ride with Ramirez until it's fixed," Chief Price said.

"That stupid twerp! Looks like he'll definitely dry out this time," Celebrity said.

"I'll come to visit you sometime today," the chief said. He really wanted to hang up and get Dr. Canada on the phone as well as Jimmy before he visited her.

Chief Price had Dr. Canada paged and explained the situation. The doctor told him he'd evaluate his patient and let the chief know how he would proceed. Next, the chief called Jimmy. "Where are you?"

"I thought I'd go visit Celebrity before I came by your office," Jimmy said, as he brought a clean bowl of water to Guppy's holder on the fake tree. He listened to the chief and heard the angst in his voice.

"Don't bring up any mention of those two kids or anything else Celebrity mentioned before," Chief Price said. "You can talk about what happened—that seems to be an okay subject."

"I'm so relieved to hear we don't have to keep up that fantasy life," Jimmy said. He walked over to his desk and picked up the cookbook he bought for Celebrity. "I'll bring her Rim's cookbook. That sounds like a conversation that shouldn't have any side effects."

"Sounds good. I'll catch up with you." Chief Price disconnected the call.

JIMMY ENTERED room 204 and found Celebrity sitting up in bed watching local news. "Hi Celeb."

"Jimmy! It's so good to have company," she said.

He didn't detect any possessiveness, neediness, or anything relating to him as her husband and the father to the phantom children. He breathed out a deep sigh of relief.

"You missed Rim's cookbook launch. I got you an autographed copy," he said as he handed her the cookbook.

"Oh, thanks. I wish I could have been there. Did a lot of people show up to support him?" she asked.

"Yeah, there was a crowd," Jimmy said. He glanced around the room and noticed a lot of the plants and flowers were missing. "What happened to all the plants and stuff?"

"I had them sent over to the nursing home so those people could enjoy them," Celebrity said.

"Oh, that's nice." Jimmy fidgeted. He silently prayed that nothing would crop up to tip her back into that other reality. "So, when will you get discharged?"

"Dr. Canada wants to keep me overnight to make sure the concussion is fully healed," Celebrity said. "The chief is checking with insurance to see when I can come back to work."

It was bizarre. Evidently, she didn't realize that she had been in the hospital for weeks and that the concussion was long gone. Jimmy wondered who would bring that subject up and how it would be addressed. Surely, she'd look at the calendar on her phone and discover it had been weeks since she tried to apprehend Armbruster.

"Would you want me to bring you food from the Bull Ride, Francesca's, or Four Score? Or, almost forgot, how about the Brass Elephant?"

"Oh, wow! So many choices. I sure could go for Indian food. Heavy on the saag paneer and rice. Don't forget the naan bread. Oh... and get rice pudding!" Celebrity smiled brightly at the thought of devouring one of her favorite foods.

"I'll load up so we can eat together. Be back in a little bit," Jimmy said.

Celebrity pulled her phone off the charger. It had been as dead as a doornail, and finally showed that it was fully charged. She stared at the home screen with her brows creased, almost touching with the frown she wore. She raised an eyebrow as she tapped on her sent emails. The last email she had sent was over a month ago. Not even one email or text to her mother.

"How is this possible?"

She stared off into space, trying to backtrack this lost time, but she couldn't put anything together. All she found was a big blank. She grabbed the call button and jammed her finger on it.

One nurse finally came into the room after her long wait. "What do you need, Celebrity?"

She tried to hold back her panic. "Have I been in a coma? I haven't sent any emails in almost a month!"

The nurse approached the bed and patted her patient on the shoulder. "Let me contact Dr. Canada. He will be able to explain your circumstances far better than I can." The nurse rushed out of the room. She didn't want to disclose any of the odd behavior that they had dealt with over the past few weeks. She returned to the nurses' station and paged Dr. Canada.

The doctor called the desk. "Don't divulge anything. I'll be right there."

CHAPTER FOUR

Jimmy returned with white bags loaded with food. He held them up for Celebrity to see as he walked through the door. Then noticed her frown. "What's wrong?"

"Was I in a coma or something? I just checked my phone and I haven't had any interactions with anyone for almost a month!" Celebrity's voice peaked into a panic.

Dr. Canada rushed into the room. He gave Jimmy warning eyes mentally telling him to keep his lips buttoned.

The hospital phone rang. Celebrity stared at it a moment then picked up the receiver on the second ring. "Hello? Oh, hi mom."

Hi, honey. How are you doing today? Tulip and Dorchester miss you.

"Who's that?" Celebrity asked.

Your kids, honey. You don't remember them?

"Mom, is dad there? Can I talk to him?"

Hi Celeb. What's going on?

"Dad, is mom having a nervous breakdown? She seems to

think I have two kids called Tulip and Dorchester. Who on God's green Earth would name their kids that?"

Dr. Canada approached Celebrity and wiggled his fingers, wanting the phone. She handed it to the doctor. "Mr. Masters? It's Dr. Canada. We'll call you back in a little while." He hung up the phone.

Celebrity looked from the doctor to Jimmy, who looked guilty about something, but she couldn't put a finger on it.

Dr. Canada sat on the edge of the bed and took Celebrity's hand. "Celebrity, you were in a coma for a short while, then when you came out of it you seemed to think that you and Jimmy were married and had a four-year-old daughter named Tulip, and a two-year-old son named Dorchester. A specialist explained to us that sometimes these realities are caused by gaps in time that your brain needs to fill in. You must have either read or watched something with those names."

Celebrity stared at the doctor as if he had suddenly gone nuts. Then she swung her accusing eyes over to Jimmy.

"Listen, we had everyone going along with what you made up so you wouldn't lapse back into a coma. It was crazy," Jimmy explained.

Celebrity was quiet for several moments. "I remember reading a book about a goat named Tulip." She thought hard for several more minutes. "The Dorchester is a high-rise in New York in another book. How bizarre my brain would latch onto those two names for my kids!" Then she started bawling her eyes out. "I'm so embarrassed. Everyone having to play along. Oh, Jimmy. How can I ever look at you again for what I put you through!"

She flopped onto her side and buried her face in the pillow while she cried.

Jimmy set the bags of food on the floor, then approached the bed. He patted her back while she wailed. "Celeb, it's okay.

It's what friends do when something goes wrong. Come on. It's going to be okay. Are you going to help me eat all this Indian food? I bribed them to include regular plates and promised I'd return them."

Celebrity lifted her face from the pillow. "Even my parents played along?"

"They recorded two children's voices that were playing so you'd hear them in the background," Dr. Canada admitted. "We had to do everything we could to keep you calm while your brain healed from the concussion and the following coma. Why don't you have something to eat? We can talk more later."

Dr. Canada patted her on the back and left the room.

Jimmy grabbed the bags and brought them to the wide window ledge where all the plants had been. Only one vase of beautiful flowers remained. He noticed they were from him. Jimmy emptied the bags of food, unwrapped the two plates and commenced to plate up the food. He handed Celebrity utensils wrapped in a cloth napkin then placed her plate of food on the patient tray.

He stuck his silverware and napkin into his pocket then snatched up his plate of food and sat in the visitor chair beside the bed.

Celebrity tore off a piece of naan bread and scooped up saag paneer. She moaned with pleasure.

Jimmy ate heartily. He loved Indian food.

"I can't believe you went along with this stupid story," Celebrity said.

"Well, it was a bit of a shock when you went into details about the kids, us, and everything else," he said between bites.

"No wonder the chief sounded surprised when I asked him if I could come back to work." Celebrity thought back over the conversation.

"Oh, I bet he was shocked you had returned," Jimmy said.

THREE DAYS LATER, Celebrity was back on the job after obtaining her doctor's release. She sat at her desk and looked around the room, taking in all the activity. She blushed as she wondered who knew about her crazy ordeal she had gone through. After the phone call with her parents, letting them know they didn't have to *babysit* Tulip and Dorchester anymore, she heard relief in their voices.

"We were so worried we'd have to produce these kids," her mother said. "Your father and I didn't know what to do."

"Jimmy suggested we find two kids on the internet who were running around playing, so that's what we did in case you wanted to see them," her father said. "I played the audio in the background anytime you called, just in case."

After she set that aside, she watched the footage from the ATM to see what had happened to cause her coma. That drunken idiot, Caleb Armbruster. The footage showed him walloping her in the head with the rock, then lurching toward the cruiser and driving away.

Now that she had those pieces put back together, she felt okay. There was nothing she could do about the whole fantasy episode. What she understood was that her brain needed details for that gap, and it went about creating its own little storybook. "I will never live this down," she muttered.

The phone rang, and Stephanie, their dispatcher who handled all incoming 9-1-1 calls, was on it immediately. "Twinkle police department. What is your emergency?"

I think my mother's dead! She's on the kitchen floor and she's foaming at the mouth!

"What's your name, and her name, and what happened?" Stephanie asked. She saw the address on her screen. She buzzed the chief, who walked the few paces from his office to hers and listened to the call when she placed it on speaker.

I'm Tonya Bloomhurst and my mother is Maybellene Towers. I just got here. We were supposed to go over to the Dime Water Foo and the Wellness Center. She didn't feel good. The door was locked, and she didn't answer the door when I knocked, which I thought was odd, so I let myself in and found her on the floor in the kitchen. What should I do?

"Okay, Tonya. Don't touch anything. Why don't you wait outside? The police and an ambulance will be there shortly," Stephanie said. She muted the call.

"Get the EMTs on the radio. Tell them no mouth-to-mouth. Sounds like poisoning to me," Chief Price blurted. "If I remember correctly, it could be sarin or cyanide. Those two poisons cause foaming at the mouth."

Stephanie's wide eyes acknowledged the chief, clearly shocked.

The chief waved his hand for Celebrity to follow him out the door.

When they arrived at 914 Schuster Street, the ambulance was just pulling up. A young woman rushed off the front porch and practically collided with Chief Price's chest.

"She didn't seem this sick when I talked to her just a little while ago," Tonya said, crying and stammering.

"When did you last speak with her?" the chief asked.

Tonya dug her phone out of her purse and pulled up the call and thrust the phone at the chief. "Forty-five minutes ago."

"Please wait by or inside your vehicle," Chief Price said. He popped open the trunk of his service vehicle and extracted personal protection equipment (PPE) for himself and Celebrity.

"Put on your PPE," he instructed the deputy, and he

masked, goggled, and gloved himself. Then he and Celebrity rushed into the house.

The EMTs, fully masked and wearing protective goggles, carefully lifted Mrs. Towers onto a power stretcher lowered to floor level. They started an IV, then rushed the stretcher out of the house and into the ambulance.

The chief took in the scene. An empty glass stood beside a bottle of supplements from Bill Hill's Wellness Center on the kitchen table. He assumed the poison came from the bottle but wasn't ruling out poison on the glass.

"Celebrity, bag that bottle and the glass. Double glove yourself. Make sure your mask is secured over your mouth and nose. If it's sarin, one whiff of that stuff will do you in. Grab them as close to the bottom as possible in the off-chance that there're other prints on either of them close to the top."

He pulled out his phone. "Dr. Canada? We've got a situation. Woman, approximately mid to late 50s, ingested poison or something that caused foaming at the mouth. Could be sarin or cyanide, but I'm not sure. The EMTs will bring her in. I need you to let me know as soon as humanly possible if that's the case, or if something else is going on. We're sending the bottle and glass to the lab."

We'll pump her stomach, which will go to the bacteriology and tox labs. Blood will go to the microbiology lab. I'll put a rush on them and get the results to you as soon as they're available.

"Okay, thanks." Chief Price turned to Celebrity. "Get the bottle and glass over to the lab. Tell them to stop whatever they're doing and get us results ASAP. Make sure you tell them we suspect those two poisons. We can't shut down the Wellness Center until we know for sure there's a problem, and I don't want to start a panic."

The chief followed the EMTs. He stopped Tonya from climbing into the rear of the ambulance with her mother.

"It's best you drive yourself since you aren't wearing any personal protective equipment. It could be dangerous in that enclosed space," Chief Price explained.

"Oh! Poor Mom!" Tonya exclaimed.

"Tonya, did your mom have any enemies? Do you know of anyone who would want to harm her?" the chief asked.

"Enemies?" Tonya squealed. Her mouth gaped like a fish out of water as she processed what the chief was asking. Could someone have a vendetta against her mom and want to murder her?

"My mom works the assembly line at the printer for the TIN, putting the paper together. Who would hold a grudge against her?" Tonya asked.

"Okay. Better let her boss know what's going on since she won't be at work today," the chief said. He hurried to his cruiser and sped over to Jiltson Way to the Twinkle Independent News.

Milly Montoya greeted the chief as he came through the front door.

"Are Sylvan and Bill available?" he asked her.

Milly checked the phones and nodded. She sent a quick text to each and received an all-clear. "Better hurry before someone calls. Should I hold all calls for a bit?"

"That would be great," the chief said. He walked through the staffers' desks and tables to Sylvan's office, where Bill Trance sat in front of the desk. Chief Price closed the door.

"Gentlemen, we have a problem," Chief Price stated.

"What's up, Kenton?" Sylvan asked as his feet rested on an open desk drawer.

"Do you know Maybellene Towers?" the chief asked.

"That name sounds familiar," Bill said.

"She works the assembly line putting the paper together," the chief supplied.

"Oh, that's where I heard her name before," Bill said. "What's wrong?"

"Someone poisoned her. She's on the way to the hospital," the chief said.

Sylvan dropped his feet to the floor, and he sat ramrod straight. "WHAT?"

Bill jumped to his feet, staring at Chief Price as if he were completely nuts. "What the heck happened?"

Chief Price gave the basic information, leaving out any connection to the Wellness Center.

"Do you think someone on the assembly line poisoned her? Should we halt production?" Sylvan asked.

"It's too soon to tell," the chief said. "I hope to have vital information before the day is out, then we might need to secure a larger crime scene."

Bill worked his phone. Chief Price figured he was sending someone over to the hospital to lurk about for details they could print in the next edition.

Because of a Wednesday and Saturday print timetable, the TIN always prayed news happened on their schedule. It was annoying that the radio and TV scooped them. Sylvan and Bill had discussed upping production, but that was still up in the air. Months ago, the attempted murder of Jimmy Katz, and all the other attempts on his person, pets, and at the boarding house, prompted special editions.

With the arrival of the Katz-Diaz heir in Twinkle, a crime wave came to the county seat of Starlight County, the town had never experienced anything like it in its history. Crime hadn't been this bad even when oil was booming in the early days and people were trying to grab land. The county only saw one or two serious criminal activities a year for several decades, until more recently, with drugs crossing their borders and people getting hooked.

This time, however, there was no attempt on Jimmy Katz whatsoever. This poisoning was a random act of a lunatic, the chief suspected. Until he received a call from ChemLabs.

JIMMY RETURNED from Bill Hill's store with two more bottles of Wellness In A Bottle. He set the sack on the table. Maddy jumped up on the table and hissed at the small paper bag.

"What's wrong with you? Did you wake up on the wrong side of your cushion? Cats are supposed to like bags." Jimmy reached for the bag, and Maddy whacked his hand away.

"Danger! Danger!" Guppy hollered. The Amazon parrot flew across the living room to the kitchen, snatched the bag with his clawed feet and dropped it into the kitchen trash can.

Jimmy could hardly believe his eyes. His animals had never acted so strangely before. Guppy and Maddy did work as a team in the previous attacks, but the reporter-turned-heir didn't see any connection to a crime in progress. Their behavior stumped him.

He walked over to the trash can, reached inside, and pulled out the bag. "Why don't I just put this in the pantry so you can't see it?"

Maddy looked angry.

Guppy pecked Jimmy on the back of his hand.

"OW! What'd you do that for?" Jimmy rubbed his hand and glared at his pets. "Don't make me call a pet psychiatrist!"

CHAPTER FIVE

Stomping up the stairs brought a knock on the door. Before he could say *come in*, Brian and Danny stormed through the door.

"Oh, good. You've just entered the nuthouse," Jimmy said.

The guys waited for an explanation, but none was forthcoming.

"What are these two clowns up to now?" Brian asked as he scratched Maddy's head then rubbed his hand over Guppy's feathers.

"Let's see if they'll repeat it," Jimmy said. He grabbed the sack and held it out to his friends.

Maddy jumped into action. Not only did she hiss, but she growled deeply and grabbed the bag with her teeth and tossed it across the table. At that point, Guppy took flight, snatched up the bag and, once again, deposited it in the trash can.

Everyone stood stock still as they digested what they just witnessed.

"What's in the bag?" Danny asked. All he saw was a small, plain brown paper bag.

"I picked up two more bottles of Wellness In A Bottle," Jimmy said, as he once more retrieved the bag from the trash.

Brian knocked the bag out of his hand this time. "They're trying to tell you why we came over! Mrs. Towers is in the hospital. Someone messed with her bottle of that stuff and she almost died from poison!"

"What?" Jimmy belted out. "How could Maddy and Guppy know that? They haven't even watched the news today!"

"Obviously, Maddy sensed something and told Guppy about it so they could work out a solution to protect you," Danny said.

"Better call the chief!" Brian said.

All three men grabbed their cellphones.

Jimmy held up a hand. "I'll call!" He pressed his speed dial for Chief Price. The phone rang three times before the chief answered.

"Jimmy, let me call you back later. We've got a dangerous situation we're trying to contain," Chief Price said.

"That's what I'm calling about. Danny and Brian came over. I was showing them how Maddy and Guppy were acting about the two bottles of Wellness In A Bottle in this sack..."

"DO NOT OPEN EITHER OF THOSE BOTTLES," the chief roared into the phone. "Do you have any other bottles from the Wellness Center?"

"Yes. I was feeling bad almost a month ago, and I went there and Bill sold me a couple of things, including a bottle of Wellness In A Bottle, which got me over whatever was trying to make me sick," Jimmy said. "I took three doses, which are eighteen capsules, and I got better."

"Bring all the bottles over to the Wellness Center," Chief Price said.

"Okay. I'll be there in a little while," Jimmy said. He blew out a breath as he stared at his friends. "Dodged that bullet."

The three of them turned and stared at Maddy and Guppy in awe.

Brian nodded knowingly. Danny wasn't in on the secret that passed between Brian and Jimmy. Brian's questioning eyes darted from Jimmy to Danny.

Jimmy gave a slight shake of his head. Even though he trusted Danny, he was a newspaperman first, and the newspaper was his family's business. Brian was Jimmy's friend from childhood. He trusted him completely. Even though Brian now worked at the newspaper, he would not divulge what he, Mrs. Potts, the chief, and Jimmy had witnessed from the hidden cameras during more than one break-in at Jimmy's apartment.

Jimmy snapped out of his momentary fog and headed to the pantry, where he grabbed the opened bottle. He wanted to add it to the sack but was wary of even opening the small bag.

"Better get going," he said. "The chief's waiting."

TWO CARS FOUND parking places on Andrajules Street, which was filled with police cars, hazard control vehicles, and plain black cars that were most likely FBI or other agencies. Jimmy, Brian, and Danny walked over to the Wellness Center.

People gawked from the sidewalks. They could see the proprietor, Bill Hill, standing behind the counter through the storefront windows while what looked like an army of people wandered up and down the aisles bagging things.

Danny found his father outside, along with Ag (Agatha) Diaz, who was snapping pictures.

Jimmy approached the door of the establishment and tapped on the blue doorframe. The chief opened the door and let him in. Jimmy placed the bag, and the single opened bottle on the counter. Bill Hill stood at the other end of the counter talking to someone Jimmy assumed was a federal agent.

"There can't be anything wrong with this bottle because, like I mentioned, I already took three doses—eighteen capsules," Jimmy said. He nodded at the bag. "Those, however, must be tainted." He lowered his voice to a whisper. "Maddy and Guppy nearly went ballistic... twice!"

"Danny doesn't *know*, does he?" the chief whispered.

"No, but he saw their weird behavior," Jimmy whispered.

"Do you have the receipts for these two purchases? That would help with a timeline," Chief Price said.

Jimmy extracted his wallet and dug through it. He pulled out several receipts and found the two purchases from the Wellness Center. He handed them to the chief.

Chief Price put everything in an evidence bag, filled in the details, and clearly signed his name and initialed where indicated. "We will not mention how you knew there was anything wrong with the bottles in the bag to the Feds. Just tell them your newspaper friends told you about the story they were working on, and you didn't want to take any chances."

"Good idea," Jimmy said. "We sure don't want to give them any interest in my animals."

The chief brought the bag over to an agent who seemed to be in charge. "I'd like to request these be sent to your lab for urgent processing." He inclined his chin in Jimmy's direction at the counter. "That's Jimmy Katz, the heir to the Katz-Diaz billions. Get my drift?"

The agent's face turned more serious. He took the bag. "Let me have a few words with him." They walked over to Jimmy.

He stuck out his hand to Jimmy. "Agent Wilson." They shook hands. "Tell me the story about these bottles."

"The single bottle will be missing eighteen capsules. I was

sick almost a month ago, and my landlady sent me over here to get something to make me feel better."

"Obviously, no adverse effects," Agent Wilson said. "The bag?"

"I bought two more bottles this morning to keep on hand since the stuff worked so well," Jimmy explained. "I just got home when my two coworkers showed up and told me about the story they were working on about the poisoning, so I didn't even open the paper bag... didn't want to take any chances."

Agent Wilson gave Chief Price somewhat of a glare. "Coworkers? I thought you didn't have to work."

"I'm a journalist and I live in a boarding house instead of my great-aunt's mansion, and I still write at least one story a week," Jimmy explained.

Agent Wilson stared at the heir as if he didn't understand what language was being used. "More power to you."

"Can I go now?" Jimmy asked.

"I know where to find you," Agent Wilson said, then turned and walked away. He handed the evidence bag to someone who rushed out the door.

Jimmy followed the agent out, then joined the little circle of TIN people.

"What's going on in there?" Sylvan asked. "They're not charging Bill with anything, are they?"

"Some agent is questioning him," Jimmy said. "They're going to put a rush on lab testing the bottles I bought."

"This is too much like the Chicago Tylenol murders back in 1982," Bill Trance said. "Let's hope it was only one bottle."

"Mrs. Towers hasn't died, has she?" Danny asked.

"Not as far as we know," Sylvan said.

Jimmy and Brian made eye contact. Maddy and Guppy were pretty clear about their opinions. There was something wrong with the new bottles. It was now up to the lab testing to validate those animals.

BRIAN, Jimmy, and Mrs. Potts were huddled in Jimmy's apartment talking quickly and emphatically, while Danny left to interview someone for an assignment.

"Loose lips sink ships," Mrs. Potts said. "I don't think Danny is a blabbermouth, but with this..." she flung her arms toward the living room and Guppy and Maddy, "we can't take a chance. All it would take is one slip of the tongue and word would spread. Then the government would swoop in and confiscate your pets and dissect their brains."

"Okay, we don't tell Danny anything. We stick with the original pact," Jimmy said.

Two thumps sounded on the front door downstairs. Mrs. Potts took to the stairs, followed by Jimmy and Brian. Danny stood on the porch with a wide-eyed stare.

"Danny, are you okay?" Mrs. Potts asked.

"Mrs. Towers died," he said. "And someone else is in the hospital with the same symptoms."

"Oh, no!" Mrs. Potts said. "Why don't you come in and I'll fix you a cup of tea."

Danny shook his head. "Can't. Brian, you're needed at the office. My dad is formulating a plan."

"Want me to come too?" Jimmy asked.

"Up to you," Danny said.

SYLVAN STONERICH STOOD at the front of the conference room. "We're in a much better position now than they had back in 1982. We have cellphones, texting, emails and social media."

Chief Price walked back to the conference room. He nodded to everyone and let Sylvan continue.

"We've devised a plan to use our modern technology to cover the county to try to avoid any more deaths," Sylvan said. "News and radio stations will interrupt programming to alert the public to the danger. All businesses, private or government offices in Starlight County, Twinkle and the surrounding towns with websites and email lists will get busy spreading the word."

Chief Price butted in. "Our police cruisers will hit all the streets in town, along with sheriff's department deputies and the Texas Rangers using their PA systems to alert those who don't pay much attention to social media. We're going to hit all the outlying areas."

"Are there any suspects?" Gert asked. The TIN salesperson was rail-thin and looked like she always had a question because of the way she penciled her eyebrows. "I sort of remember back in '82 they determined it wasn't anything to do with the manufacturing process. Someone bought a bunch of bottles from different stores, doctored them with poison, then went around putting them on shelves."

"No suspects yet. The Feds are looking at all videos from the surrounding area to identify everyone who set foot in the store," Chief Price said. "It's a matter of questioning and eliminating innocent people to catch the person responsible for this atrocity."

"What about Bill Hill?" Ag asked. "He may go belly up with all his inventory being confiscated."

Jimmy piped up. "My aunt and I won't let that happen. He's just an innocent bystander with a convenient store that some weasel is trying to ruin."

"Hmm," Bill Trance said. "Chief, has anyone thought that

this may be a vendetta against Bill Hill? Maybe someone is trying to get even with him for something?"

"I'm sure the Feds have thought about that, but I'll mention it to Agent Wilson. There's no telling what this is about," Chief Price said.

Jimmy had a thought. He figured he'd better wait until he and Brian were alone, then he could share his wild solution with the chief.

JIMMY AND BRIAN showed up at the boarding house relatively on time for supper. As they settled into their chairs, Jimmy blurted out his thoughts to his pact-mates.

"I had a thought when the chief said the Feds were looking at videos of anyone who set foot inside the Wellness Center." He eyed Mrs. Potts and Brian.

"Spit it out, dude," Brian said.

"I bet Maddy and Guppy could identify the killer. If we could get all that footage from cameras on both sides of the street, they could watch it and probably let us know who did this."

Mrs. Potts and Brian quietly digested Jimmy's suggestion.

"That's not a bad idea," Mrs. Potts said. "We all know Maddy understands language on more than a basic level to be able to communicate on the computer. Even Guppy knows when and how to take action. They may be able to easily identify the culprit."

"Would the chief be able to get that footage if the Feds won't share?" Brian asked.

"Let me send him a text," Jimmy said. He pulled his cell phone out.

Chief, would you have time for a short PACT meeting?

Several long moments passed while everyone ate meatloaf, mashed potatoes, and peas before Jimmy's phone dinged an incoming message.

Be there after dinner.

Everyone nodded. They might have a solid plan. After they finished supper, the table was cleared and the dishwasher was loaded. They went about their business, waiting for the chief.

Twenty minutes later, Chief Price knocked on the boarding house door. Mrs. Potts let him in. Brian and Jimmy joined them in the kitchen. It was one of those rare times they saw the chief in street clothes.

"First, I think you should look at the camera footage leading up to what happened today. Just don't let Maddy see it. I think it's best to keep this secret from her so we can catch her and Guppy in action," Jimmy said.

"This I can't wait to see," the chief said. He had been floored when the secret cameras upstairs captured Jimmy's smart kitten grabbing a pencil in her mouth and whacking keys to send a message when the invader broke into the apartment.

The group climbed the stairs and entered the apartment. After everyone greeted Maddy and Guppy, they talked about random things so the animals would go about their business. Then the pact group gathered around the computer while Jimmy pulled up the footage from the morning.

Everyone watched Maddy and Guppy act out over the paper bag. The chief rocked on his heels, thoughts pouring through his head.

"Why don't we go downstairs for a nice cup of tea," Mrs. Potts said.

CHAPTER SIX

"Does anyone really want tea, or should we just talk?" Mrs. Potts asked, as everyone sat at the table.

"Let's talk," the chief said, as he nodded to Jimmy. "What did you have in mind?"

"We think Maddy and Guppy could identify this person if they watched all the video footage the Feds gathered," Jimmy said.

"Look, we know it sounds crazy, but we're talking about two sentient, intelligent creatures who, through their ability to communicate with the human world, have already averted disaster by saving Jimmy multiple times," Brian said.

"Kenton, we have to try this," Mrs. Potts said.

"It's an excellent idea," the chief said. "There's one problem, though, and it won't be easy to overcome. Once they identify the suspect, how do we legally have him arrested? It's not like Maddy and Guppy can take the stand."

"We'll have to think about that, but in the meantime, get the footage and have them watch it," Jimmy said.

Mrs. Potts held her hand out, palm down. "Keep the pact."

Brian, Jimmy, and the chief piled their hands on top of hers.

"I feel guilty not telling Danny and Celebrity," Jimmy said.

"Keep the circle small," Chief Price said. "Too much is at risk."

Mrs. Potts patted Jimmy on the shoulder. "It's a great responsibility to keep this huge secret. We have to protect the animals at all costs."

The chief stood. "I'd better get back home. I'll let you know when I get video footage."

Mrs. Potts walked the chief to the door.

"Want to go out to the gazebo?" Jimmy asked Brian.

"Sure. Let's grab a couple of brewskis," Brian suggested.

"I'll get Maddy and Guppy," Jimmy said. He left the kitchen and climbed the stairs. "Who wants to take the basket express out to the gazebo?"

"Freedom!" Guppy belted out. His parrot lungs were capable of competing with a foghorn.

Jimmy went to the pantry, grabbed Maddy's basket, a kitchen towel, and a couple of beers. Maddy hopped into the basket. Guppy landed on Jimmy's towel-protected arm. They met Brian at the back door, then walked across the lawn to the screened-in gazebo Mrs. Potts' nephews had built.

Brian latched the door after them. Maddy hopped out of the basket onto the bench, and Guppy fluttered up to the ledge to scope out the trees for attack squirrels.

Jimmy's phone dinged a text from Danny.

Where are you?

Jimmy texted back: gazebo.

K. On my way.

"Danny's here," Jimmy said.

A few minutes later, Danny joined them inside. "Hey. Got another beer?"

Jimmy handed over his extra beer.

"Bill Hill just left his store. He looked so dejected," Danny said, then twisted off the bottle cap and took a swig.

"Did the Feds take all his inventory, or were they focusing on the Wellness In A Bottle?" Jimmy asked.

"My dad and I watched them. It seemed to be a very methodical process. I think they must have used a numbering system for the rows and shelves, maybe even the location," Danny said. "Nothing's left. Just bare shelves."

"There's probably a psychological purpose to that—where a tainted bottle was for customers to grab. Most stores have stockers to pull inventory to the front, so nothing expires from being shoved to the back," Brian said.

"Does Bill have stockers?" Jimmy asked.

"I think so, but not really sure. Maybe he did everything himself," Danny said.

"Since they never caught that Tylenol killer, I don't think they have any psychological data from that whole debacle," Brian said.

"Yeah, but technology has developed to the point where I don't know how anyone could get away with this today," Jimmy said. "All the cameras that track everyone coming and going, order delivery tracking, and all the rest of it."

"Are there cameras in the store?" Danny asked.

"I didn't think to look for any when I was in there," Jimmy said, disappointed in himself.

"Won't his insurance cover the loss of his inventory?" Brian asked.

They all thought about it.

"Not sure how a policy would be worded for a crime like this in a retail store," Danny said.

"I bet my aunt or DDS would know," Jimmy said. "I'll ask her tomorrow."

DANNY CALLED Jimmy first thing in the morning. "Dude, someone from Jupiter didn't make it to the hospital."

Jimmy practically ran down the stairs to the kitchen. His landlady was flipping through a circular as she sipped coffee.

"Mrs. Potts! There's been another poisoning! Someone from Jupiter!"

"Oh, no!" Mrs. Potts said.

"Doesn't sound like the plan worked," Danny said over Jimmy's speakerphone.

"What plan?" Mrs. Potts asked.

"The cops were going to cover neighborhoods and outlying areas using their PA systems, and all businesses were going to send emails and use other means to contact people," Jimmy said.

"Who could have done such a monstrous thing?" Mrs. Potts wailed.

"I'd better go." Danny clicked off.

"I'm going to get dressed, then go see my aunt," Jimmy said.

"Tell her I said hello," Mrs. Potts said.

Jimmy rushed out of the kitchen, up the stairs, and into his bathroom. When he was dressed and ready to head out with his gun strapped inside his shoulder holster and hidden by his jacket, he sat on the sofa.

"Maddy, Guppy, remember the bad paper bag? People have died from the bad bag. The cops don't know who did it. We have to help find the bad person who is killing people," Jimmy said. He tried to keep his language simple so that they would understand. "I'm going to see Aunt Betty. Be back later."

Maddy yawned and hunkered down on her cushion while Guppy kept up squirrel surveillance.

JENKINS ANSWERED THE DOOR. "Good morning, Jimmy. Your aunt is in the conservatory this morning." He closed the door after Jimmy stepped into the mansion and walked him back.

Jimmy saw his aunt touching plants while talking. He whispered, "Jenkins, is she talking to the plants, or is she talking to someone with her Bluetooth?"

"Oh, she's talking to the plants this morning." Jenkins winked at Jimmy, then left him at the conservatory doorway.

"Hi Aunt Betty. Is everyone in here okay this morning?" Jimmy asked.

"Hello Jimmy. Yes, all the plants are doing okay now that they're over the shock of losing one of their relatives. I tried to root an avocado seed in water, but it rotted. We'll try again in the kitchen or my office. I won't let them see one of their own fail."

Jimmy stared at his aunt for a moment, at a loss for words.

"They're alive, Jimmy. They communicate," Betty said.

Jimmy pecked her on the cheek. "I know they're alive. Aunt Betty, you've heard about what's happened at the Wellness Center, haven't you?"

She laced her arm through his and led him to her office. "Yes, terrible business, this poisoning."

"I don't know how Bill's insurance works, whether they will cover his confiscated inventory or not," Jimmy said.

"I'm one step ahead of you, Jimmy. DDS is checking into that. Whatever the insurance company doesn't pay for Bill's claim, we'll supply the balance through one of our charitable organizations," Betty said. "If the policy has any clauses or loopholes whereby they won't honor the claim because of criminal activity, we'll cover what they don't. I believe Stoney has already contacted Bill."

"He's an innocent bystander and shouldn't be forced to take out a loan for inventory. The shelves are bare, Aunt Betty," Jimmy said.

"The important thing right now is to find whoever did this. Unfortunately, there may be more deaths or hospitalizations because people won't follow directions. The warning has been on TV, radio, all social media channels, and has been blasted out on everyone's email lists. I've handed over my stash of products," Betty said.

"Yeah, the one time people need to pay attention, they flake out, which could end up killing them. I think I'm going to head over to the TIN and see what else is new." Jimmy hugged his aunt and left.

As he drove the short distance, he saw one of the patrol cars creeping down the street. The air stirred with the sound of the PA system blaring the warning to bring all purchases from the Wellness Center to the police station. He turned down Jiltson Way and entered the driveway for the Twinkle Independent News' rear parking lot, got out of his car and entered through the employee door.

Danny, Brian, Kingston (Deuce) Bainbridge, the sports editor, and Eddie Garcia, the production, tech support and website guy, were huddled, whispering. Jimmy joined them.

"What's going on?" Jimmy whispered as he slipped into a chair and rolled up to the table.

"Two deaths, and three more people in the hospital," Danny said.

"We're going to put out a special edition, and I've updated the website," Eddie said.

"Didn't they hear the news?" Jimmy blurted. "I can't believe people are so careless with their lives!"

"They're going to do what they want to do," Deuce said. He shrugged.

Sylvan's door opened. He and Bill Trance came out and walked over to the group.

"Okay, here's the plan. Eddie, you'll keep the website up to date even if you have to stay up all night. Deuce, there's not much going on sports-wise at the moment, so I want you to help with human-interest stories. Five people have been affected. Their lives, their families, loved ones, businesses, jobs, coworkers, associations, and acquaintances. This poisoning spreads wide," Sylvan said.

"Jimmy, can you help Danny and Brian? I'll take one of the stories," Bill Trance said.

"You bet. The police are still spreading the word with their cruisers," Jimmy said. "Any word from the Feds or Chief Price? Does anyone know what's going on with the search for the murderer?"

"I'm going to talk to the chief and see if the lab has found more contaminated bottles. People are dropping off their purchases at the police station, so at least something is happening. I want to know why all the inventory was confiscated. I thought just Wellness In A Bottle contained poison," Sylvan said.

"People, have your stories in my inbox before the night is over," Bill Trance said.

Jimmy was assigned to interview family, friends and loyal customers of Beulah Mae Greenhorn, owner of the Biggem Diner. She was hospitalized mid-morning when she collapsed at work. First stop was the hospital to find out if he was memorializing her, or writing a different piece. He hoped she pulled through.

He entered through the front door and approached the

desk. "Can you tell me what room Beulah Mae Greenhorn is in?"

"She's in the ICU," the attendant said. "No visitors unless you're family, and I know you're not family."

"Who can tell me her status? I'm writing an article for the TIN," Jimmy pleaded.

"Doctor Canada is tied up. I'll see if Doctor Grotski is available."

Jimmy waited patiently while the doctor was paged.

Justin Grotski didn't look like any doctor Jimmy had ever met. The six-footer stood out with his below the shoulder, dark brown hair that was tied back; then there was the bright blue streak on the right side. Round black studs adorned his ears, and what looked like a tattoo that peeked out from his white doctor coat's left sleeve.

"Hi, you paged me?" he said.

"Uh, yes," Jimmy stammered.

He held out his hand. "Doctor Grotski. How may I help you?"

They shook hands. The young doctor looked to be about Jimmy's age. "Jimmy Katz. I'm doing an article for the TIN, and I'd like to know what you can tell me about Mrs. Greenhorn."

Dr. Grotski steered them a couple of feet away from the desk. "There's not much I can tell you because of HIPPA (Health Insurance Portability and Accountability Act) guidelines, since you're not family. This is my first poisoning case of this type. Dr. Canada might be able to fill in the blanks," Dr. Grotski said.

"Okay. I'll try to hunt down her family, or I'll ask Dr. Canada when he has some free time," Jimmy said.

Dr. Grotski hurried away, and Jimmy pondered the situation. As he was about to leave the hospital, Dr. Canada appeared down the hallway. Jimmy caught up with him and asked about Mrs. Greenhorn.

"She was brought in through the emergency room after collapsing at the diner. Since she didn't foam at the mouth, we didn't connect her condition with the poison, but within a few minutes the symptoms became obvious," Dr. Canada said.

"Do you have any idea why there was a delay with her foaming at the mouth?" Jimmy asked.

"No idea at this time," Dr. Canada said.

"The desk said she's in the ICU. Is there any chance she might not make it?" Jimmy asked.

"There are a few underlying conditions that make it tougher to overcome this poisoning," the doctor said.

"Anything you can mention?" Jimmy asked.

Dr. Canada shook his head. "HIPPA."

"I understand. Thanks, Dr. Canada," Jimmy said. "I'll let you get back to it." He left the hospital and headed over to the Biggem Diner. The parking lot was packed. Jimmy had to park over by the dumpster. He hoped it wasn't trash day for the diner.

He walked around to the front door and entered the establishment. The place was abuzz with talk about the proprietor. Bert, the second in command and head cook, was busy taking care of customers up front, while one of the short-order cooks took over the grill.

Bert greeted Jimmy. "Seating is first come, first serve. You might have to join someone if you can find a vacant chair."

Jimmy looked around. He spotted Danny and Brian and headed to their table. "Is that my chair?" He dipped his chin toward a chair holding Danny's foot.

"Figured you'd show up since you're covering Mrs. Green-horn," Danny said. He kicked the chair out toward his pal.

"Thanks," Jimmy said. "I met with Dr. Grotski. Have you

ever met him? Long hair with a blue streak, black earplugs... not your typical looking doctor-type."

"Yeah, we hang out when he has a free couple of hours," Danny said.

"I was just surprised when I met him. Didn't expect to see someone like him at a country hospital. People blend in more in The Big City," Jimmy said.

"Have you had a chance to talk with Celebrity since she more or less came back?" Danny asked.

Brian kicked Danny's chair. "Don't be a jerk. She didn't go anywhere. It was pretty tragic when you think about it—going into a coma, then coming back with amnesia and another reality in her head. Some people never remember who they are."

"Geeze, I'm just asking a general question. I'm not making fun of the situation," Danny said.

"To answer your question, no. I have not talked to her lately. She's been tied up with this poison fiasco," Jimmy said. He looked around the diner. "Do I have to go to the counter to order? I don't see the server."

"They're short-staffed. Go up to the cash register and place your order," Brian said.

CHAPTER SEVEN

JIMMY HUNG around the Biggem Diner until the crowd thinned, then caught Bert sitting at the counter slurping a coffee.

"Hi, Bert. I know you've been swamped with Mrs. Greenhorn in the hospital. I'm writing an article about her, but I don't really know anything about her. What can you tell me?"

"Most people only see her in action where she's belting out orders and keeping people real. But she's a woman who seeks justice. There was this guy last week who came in for lunch and didn't leave the windows down enough for his dog. I thought she was going to beat him to the ground. We heard a dog crying and barking. She went outside and saw a dog desperately scratching at the car window. It must have been a hundred outside, which means it was probably 120 in that car!" Bert shook his head, reliving the experience.

"Beulah tried all four doors, but the car was locked. She came back inside and roared out, 'Who has a dog in a black car?' This guy waved his hand in the air while he was eating a sandwich. She ripped him out of his chair and practically threw him at the door, yelling for him to get his dog out of there right now!"

"I can see that happening. She's a big woman," Jimmy said. "Did he bring the dog inside?"

"Yeah, she had me get him a bowl of water. That poor dog practically sucked it dry. We got out a fan and put the dog in front of it to cool him down. Haven't seen that guy since," Bert said.

"Does she have grown kids?" Jimmy asked.

"She's got two kids, Floyd and Veronica. They're up in Austin in college. I called Floyd and told him what had happened. He was supposed to call Ronnie. Pretty sure they're at the hospital," Bert said.

"Can you ask them to call me?" Jimmy asked. He shared his phone number with Bert. "What about charities?"

"We bring food to the food bank twice a week," Bert said.

"I hope she pulls through!" Jimmy said. "I'd like to get to know her better."

Jimmy left Bert to his well-deserved break. He snapped a picture of the Biggem Diner sign, walked back to find his vehicle unassaulted, but a little stinky by the dumpster, and drove off.

MRS. POTTS ANSWERED THE DOOR. "Hello, Celebrity. You here to see Jimmy?"

The deputy, dressed in off-duty clothes, came inside. "Is he in?"

"Go on up," Mrs. Potts said, as she closed the front door to the boarding house, then returned to the kitchen.

Celebrity took off up the stairs and knocked on Jimmy's door.

After a long moment, the door swung open.

"Oh, hi, Celebrity. Come in. Make yourself at home while I finish typing this article real quick. I've got a deadline for a special edition of the TIN."

Jimmy rushed back to his desk, his fingers flying over the keyboard. Celebrity came inside, wandered into the living room and settled on the sofa. Maddy leapt onto the sofa and snuggled down into her lap, purring up a storm.

"Well, Maddy, make yourself comfy," Celebrity joked.

Not one to be left out of the action, Guppy fluttered from his tree for three whole feet, then walked across the back of the sofa until he was in back of the deputy. His beak burrowed into her hair.

"Guppy! Quit that!" Celebrity squealed as the parrot groomed her hair.

Jimmy jumped up and crossed the room to the sofa. He grabbed Guppy and brought him back to his tree. "Any more of that and I'll put you in your travel cage."

"Jealous!" Guppy squawked.

Jimmy thumped him on the beak. "Yes, you are." He turned to his visitor. "Sorry about that. I'll be done in a couple of minutes. I just need to read the story over and make sure I'm not leaving anything out."

"Can I read it?" Celebrity asked.

"Sure. You can be my proofreader. I'll print a copy." He returned to his desk, printed the story two-sided, grabbed two pens and joined Celebrity on the sofa. He handed her a pen and the story. "You read first, then I'll see what you find."

They sat quietly, reading. She circled a couple of things, wrote a note, added a comma, deleted a double word, added an end quote, then handed the pages to Jimmy.

"Oh, good catches." Jimmy read and added his own marks. "Be right back." He returned to his desk, made the corrections, added a paragraph, saved the file, then emailed it to Bill Trance. "Done!" He returned to the sofa, flopped down and turned to Celebrity.

"Would you like a beer or a glass of wine?"

"I'll take a glass of wine," she said.

He got their beverages. "So, what brings you my way?"

Celebrity turned to face him on the sofa. "I wanted to talk about our little fake family."

"There's nothing to talk about. Really. I'm just glad you came out of the coma and recovered from the amnesia," Jimmy said.

"You've been on my mind a lot ever since you moved here," Celebrity said.

Jimmy noticed her face coloring. "To be honest, you've been on my mind a lot as well. Ever since I first met you at the police station. I was going to ask you out when stupid Caleb knocked you into a coma."

"You were? Why'd you wait so long?" she asked.

"You could have asked me out, you know," he said.

She fidgeted. "I know, but it's always best if the boy asks the girl, otherwise the girl doesn't know if he's really into her."

He thought about that, then nodded. "That makes sense. I'm asking you now. Will you come to dinner with me tomorrow night? I'll pick you up."

Celebrity blushed redder, petted Maddy, and tried to steady her breathing. "Yes. Dinner sounds great. Where do you want to go?"

"Would you like to go to Francesca's? I've only been there at lunch, but the food is good," Jimmy said.

"Francesca's it is. What time?"

"I'll pick you up at seven."

JIMMY DRESSED SEMI-CASUALLY IN JEANS, t-shirt, and a sports jacket to conceal his shoulder holster. He rang the doorbell at Celebrity's apartment and forced himself not to pace or fidget. Jimmy practically fell through the door when she opened it. He teetered on his heels on the doorstep.

He visually approved of her form-fitting jeans and a scooped-neck short-sleeved shirt before he uttered a word. "Hi. You look nice."

"Want to come in for a minute?" she asked.

"Sure," he said as he stepped over the threshold.

The place was furnished for comfort. An overstuffed sofa and matching chair with reading lamps on end tables. A wall of stuffed bookcases. Large TV on the wall. A bunch of DVDs in a stand with more stacked on the floor under the bottom shelf.

"I like your place," Jimmy said.

"Me too," she said. "Maybe we should get going. There might be a lot of people for dinner."

They both seemed to charge for the door and practically collided.

"Oh, sorry," Jimmy said. He opened the door, turned her door lock. "Do you have your keys?"

She held up her keys. He closed the door, then tested that it was locked. They walked to his car, and he opened her door and closed it once she was settled and had secured her seatbelt. He jogged around the car and got inside, belted up, then they were off. Jimmy pulled into Francesca's parking area, where around a dozen cars were parked.

"See, it's filling up," Celebrity said.

They walked into the restaurant and waited to be seated. He saw Brian with someone he didn't know. When he and his friend made eye contact, Jimmy shook his head slightly. He didn't want to share his date with anyone. Brian gave him the thumbs-up sign with a huge smile.

The greeter arrived back at her stand. "Welcome to Francesca's. Two for dinner?"

"Yes," Jimmy and Celebrity said at the same time.

The greeter checked her table chart, grabbed two menus, and asked them to follow her.

Jimmy was relieved that she sat them across the room from Brian and his date. He pulled out Celebrity's chair, then seated himself across from her. They accepted the menus, then the greeter took off.

They studied their choices and were ready when the server arrived at the table. Jimmy settled on the pork tenderloin with roasted potatoes in a garlic and parmesan sauce, and a side salad. Celebrity chose tender chicken, mashed potatoes and a side salad. They both decided on iced tea.

Jimmy looked around at the diners. "Have you ever thought about eating food? We seem to make such a big production of it."

"What do you mean?" Celebrity curiously thought about what he said.

"Think about how the original humans survived. When they transitioned from plants, nuts and berries to probably watching animals eat meat. They must have given that some thought, don't you think? Then they went around learning to hunt, eating raw meat until fire was discovered."

She nodded. "Someone had to be in charge of keeping the fire alive until they learned how to start a fire from scratch. They must have had a lot to figure out with cooking food." Celebrity looked around the restaurant at all the diners, eating food, drinking beverages. "My parents will be back in Twinkle next week."

"Are they from here? I don't really know anything about them, or you, for that matter," Jimmy said.

"They temporarily moved up to the Dallas area when

Grandma Masters' health began to decline. She passed away earlier this year, and my folks have been dealing with her estate."

"Oh, I'm sorry to hear that. What will they do for work if they move back? Do they have jobs up there?" Jimmy asked.

She stared at him a moment and realized he didn't know her background. "Um, my mother is a Diaz, and my father oversees several organizations for the *empire*. Haven't you seen his name on any of the charts?"

Jimmy's chair abruptly scooted back. "We're... cousins?"

Celebrity waved a hand in the air, dismissing his shock. "Like Moses Diaz, who explains how he's X times removed from Clemento and Betty. We're not even considered kissing cousins, Jimmy."

"Oh! That's good." He was relieved to dismiss any thoughts of improper connections regarding dating.

Thankfully, their food was delivered so they could shelve the family discussion for the time being. They ate in silence for several minutes.

"This is great," Celebrity said. "How's your food?"

"Yeah, I really like their food. I'm glad we came here," Jimmy said. He harrumphed. "It's very difficult not to talk about work and police business."

"It's what we do. I'm a cop and you report things," she said. "Plus, you're friends with the chief, and because of your close connection with Betty, you get all the inside news before anyone else. What'd you want to talk about?"

"I'm bothered by this whole poisoning debacle. At first, the focus was on Wellness In A Bottle, but the feds removed the entire inventory from Bill Hill's store," Jimmy said.

"I know. Doesn't seem right to me either, but they must have a reason. Maybe they think it's not just Wellness In A Bottle and don't want to take a chance." She sipped tea, daintily patted her lips with the cloth napkin, then dug into her salad with gusto.

Jimmy smiled. "I like that you're not afraid to eat a meal."

Celebrity waved her fork at him. "I've never been one of those starvers. I'm lucky that my body doesn't store fat, but I realize that could catch up with me when I'm middle-aged."

"You look great—better than anyone I've ever dated," he said, caught up in her eyes.

She blushed furiously. "Oh, thank you. How nice of you to notice."

"I'd have to be blind..."

Suddenly, there was someone standing beside their table. "Are you enjoying yourselves? I don't recall seeing either of you here for dinner before."

They startled and looked away from each other to notice the chef.

"We love the way you prepare food here," Celebrity blurted for both of them.

"I had only been here for lunch, so this is a treat," Jimmy said.

"Would you mind if I snapped a picture of the three of us?" the chef asked. "I'd like to add it to our wall of fame." He pointed to the far wall, which was covered in photos of famous guests that included the town matriarch, politicians, wealthy families, and the occasional movie star.

They moved their chairs closer, and the chef scrunched down between them with his cellphone, and posed for a selfie. He straightened up and looked at the picture.

"Came out great. Want a copy?"

"Sure," they both said.

The chef wandered away to visit with someone else.

"Well, that was interesting," Jimmy said. "Do we wait for the server to bring us the bill, or do we go up to the front?"

"We wait," Celebrity said.

The server returned with the guest check holder and placed it in front of Jimmy. "Can I get you anything else?"

"No, we're good, thanks," Jimmy said, as he fished his wallet out of his inside jacket pocket. He pulled out a hundred-dollar bill and slipped it inside the holder. "Keep the change."

Jimmy stood, helped Celebrity with her chair, and they left. Within minutes, they were at her front door. What started as a sweet kiss soon heated. Celebrity pushed Jimmy's chest to disengage, flustered.

"I'd better go inside. Have to get ready for work tomorrow." She stopped herself from babbling more nonsense.

"Thanks for coming out with me tonight," Jimmy said. "I had a great time."

"I'll see you tomorrow?" She realized she posed that as a question like a stalker wannabe instead of it being a casual statement.

"Yes, I'll see you tomorrow." He said firmly, as if staking a claim on her.

Celebrity forced herself to turn, unlock the door and slipped inside her apartment. She used the door to stay upright as she patted her chest.

Wow! She mouthed. She peeked out the side window and watched as Jimmy got into his car and drove away.

CHAPTER EIGHT

THE CAR DROVE JIMMY HOME. He was positive it knew the route by heart because he found himself parked in front of the boarding house and didn't recall the drive home. He was still sitting in his car when Brian's car pulled up in back of him.

Brian tapped on Jimmy's window. "You okay?"

Jimmy jumped in his seat, realized he was acting like a love-struck numbskull, and opened his car door. "Sorry, just thinking," he mumbled.

Brian studied his best friend. "About... marriage and babies? You're totally hooked by the looks of it."

"I've wanted to ask her out from the first moment I saw her at the police station when I first moved here," Jimmy admitted. "We finally had our first date tonight." He gave Brian a questioning look. "Who were you with? I didn't know you were dating anyone."

"Lena Morales. I met her over at the Foo when I picked up milk for Mrs. Potts," Brian said.

"Is she a keeper?" Jimmy asked.

Brian shrugged. "Not sure. We don't seem to have much in common."

"What do you mean? She couldn't hold a conversation?" Jimmy asked.

"No, it was a little awkward. She recognized practically everyone in the restaurant," Brian said.

"So? If she's lived here all her life, she would know everyone. Twinkle's a small town," Jimmy said. "Is she related to the Morales' who made their fortune in booze?"

Brian thought about it. "Not sure. We didn't share much personal information. Guess we need to go out again."

They walked to the house, climbed the few steps. Brian unlocked the door, and they walked down the hall to the kitchen. Mrs. Potts sat at the table with a cup of coffee. She was just disconnecting a call on the house phone when the men entered the room.

"Hi Mrs. Potts," they said together. They noticed she didn't seem her regular upbeat self.

"What's wrong?" Jimmy asked.

"Has someone else been poisoned?" Brian asked.

"It's worse. The Feds have shut down the Jiltson Clinic and their online business," Mrs. Potts said.

"What for?" Jimmy asked.

"The ingredients for Wellness In A Bottle, the manufacturing and bottling were from Jiltson's natural herbs and formulas," Mrs. Potts said.

"Oh, no!" Jimmy said.

"Why would they do that?" Brian asked. "If this poisoner is going by the 1982 case, that poisoner bought the bottles from stores all around Chicago. There was nothing wrong with the manufacturing facility."

"What has become of our little town?" Mrs. Potts wailed.

"I think someone has a vendetta against Bill Hill," Jimmy said. "None of this makes much sense. The people poisoned seem random."

"Does he sell online?" Brian asked. "If so, people could be poisoned from all over the country, not just from Starlight County."

Mrs. Potts and Jimmy groaned.

"I'm pretty sure the Feds would have looked into that first. They most likely would have shut down his website and collected any online orders over a certain period," Mrs. Potts said.

Maddy batted a bottle cap across the floor.

"Is Guppy upstairs?" Jimmy asked.

"He's in his sleep cage," Mrs. Potts said. "Did you two have a good dinner with your dates?"

"Is Lena Morales related to the booze family?" Brian asked.

"Yes, she's Amelia Morales' granddaughter. You didn't know that?" Mrs. Potts asked.

Brian shook his head.

"Do you like her? If so, you need to share background information and get to know each other," Mrs. Potts suggested.

"I had no idea," Brian said.

"Go to the library," Jimmy said. "There're a couple of books that have prominent family information. That way you'll know who's who."

"Like you knew anything about Celebrity, with the exception she's a cop," Brian chided.

"You're right. I had no idea she was a Diaz," Jimmy said.

"I'm pretty sure Betty would have warned you off if Celebrity were a close cousin," Mrs. Potts said.

Both Jimmy's and Brian's phones sounded an incoming text.

"Early meeting tomorrow. Probably about the clinic being shut down," Brian said.

"See you tomorrow, Mrs. Potts," Jimmy said. "Maddy, let's go upstairs."

Maddy took off out of the kitchen, down the hall, and zoomed up the stairs.

"I wish I had that energy," Mrs. Potts said.

A HUGE THUNDERSTORM paused over Twinkle during the night. Jimmy woke in the middle of the night with Maddy practically sleeping on his head. He got up and went into the living room to make sure Guppy was okay. He shielded the sleep cage with the special cover that left the doorway open, then he trudged back to bed.

The thunder was so loud, and the sky lit up with lightning to where he couldn't go back to sleep.

His phone dinged a text from Celebrity.

I can't sleep through this storm!

He texted back. *Me neither. Heard about the Jiltson Clinic being shut down.*

She texted back: *We have to sort this out before more people die! Who would do something like this?*

Jimmy thought for a moment. *Someone who gets off on others' suffering. Not much different from our former murdering librarian. Who would have thought?*

A few minutes passed in silence. Jimmy wondered if Celebrity had fallen back asleep. Then another text came through.

You're right. Never in my wildest imagination would I have thought that scenario would occur in Twinkle! This makes me look at everyone I pass with suspicion. I don't like feeling this way.

He nodded as he read her text. *Two prominent businesses shut down. Seems to me like a pattern is forming. It's three o'clock! I've got a 7:30 meeting at the TIN, so I'd better try to get to sleep. You'll most likely have a full day as well.*

He saw her typing, then her text came through. *You're right. It's most likely going to be busy. See you later. Night.*

Night, he typed. He put his phone on the charger, then fell back onto his pillow, conking Maddy, who whacked him. "Oops. Sorry, honey. Go back to sleep. Daddy's beat."

THERE WERE several bleary-eyed people in the TIN conference room. Bill Trance handed out assignments.

"Ag, find out if there's any storm damage to report. That was something else last night. Jimmy, get over to the police station and see if you can weasel out any details about the clinic. Danny, I want you and Brian to hit up the Biggem Diner and the other restaurants to get the scuttlebutt on what people are saying about these closings. Deuce, find out if there're any sports cancellations because of the storm."

Sylvan entered the conference room. "People, those were great articles in the special edition. Jimmy, Beulah Mae Greenhorn called me in tears. I've had nothing but praise from our readers."

Jimmy piped up. "Celebrity and I were talking this morning, and it appeared to me that a pattern seems to be forming."

"What do you mean?" Sylvan asked.

"There are five prestigious families in Starlight County. One of whose businesses is shut down that is directly connected to the first business to be closed by the Feds."

The room was silent while everyone thought about what Jimmy said.

"Do you think someone is actually out to get the Jiltsons, but went about it in a way to throw suspicion off?" Bill Trance asked.

Jimmy shrugged. "I'm not sure, but it seems reasonable to suspect that, don't you think?"

"Talk to the chief about it," Sylvan said.

"Have the Jiltson's ever been sued by someone? Maybe something they sold hurt someone?" Brian threw out there.

"Look that up, Brian. It might not have made the news," Bill said.

"Okay, everyone get moving," Sylvan said.

JIMMY HEADED over to the police station. He was disappointed that he didn't see Celebrity, but was waved back to the chief's office by Sgt. Gonzales. He found Celebrity looking over the chief's shoulder at his screen.

"Anything new?" Jimmy asked as he slipped into a chair in front of the chief's desk.

"We're following up on your idea of a pattern," Chief Price said as he pulled his eyes away from the screen. "I'm looking for any criminal activity related to the Jiltsons, then I'll talk to DDS."

"You should call Aunt Betty. If anyone knows about any scandals, I would think it would be her," Jimmy said.

The chief stood. "Let's pay her a visit."

TWO CRUISERS and Jimmy's car pulled up at the mansion on Diaz Circle. Jenkins didn't seem surprised at the impromptu visitors. The butler took everything in stride.

"She's on the shooting range with Toombs," Jenkins reported.

Jimmy led the chief and Celebrity to the back of the property where Betty aimed her lucky piece, a Ruger GP100 10mm automatic, at the target. She might be in her 90s, but the modern-day Annie Oakley never, ever missed a target.

They walked with Toombs, who had retrieved the target and was on his way to the sharpshooter standing under the umbrella.

"Chief, what brings you my way?" Betty asked as the group approached.

"Hi, Aunt Betty," Jimmy said.

Toombs handed over the target with the enormous hole in the middle of the bullseye.

"Wow. I want to be able to shoot like that," Celebrity said.

"Me too," Jimmy said.

"You already shoot like that, according to Toombs," Betty said.

"I think it's genetic," Toombs said. He glanced at Celebrity. "You most likely would qualify for the club."

"Betty, do you recall any scandals regarding the Jiltsons or their business?" Chief Price asked.

"Well, there was the Henderson tragedy forty years ago," Betty said, without missing a beat.

Chief Price stared at her with his face scrunched in thought. "I don't recall that. What happened?"

"How could you? What were you—ten years old?" Betty asked. "Billy Boyd Henderson sued Trembo Jiltson after his wife committed suicide using his herbal remedies. This was long before the online store. The suit was thrown out of court.

The jury decided there was no way that Trembo could know what Susan Henderson wanted the herbs for, and he had not instructed her on how the combination of herbs she took could lead to her death."

"I'll see if DDS has the transcripts," Chief Price said. "Was there a suicide note?"

"You won't find one in the file, but there was an ugly note." Betty shook her head.

"Wait, how do you know there was a note if it wasn't in the file?" Celebrity asked, just as Jimmy opened his mouth to ask the same thing.

"Let's just say I suspected something and hired someone to find it," Betty said. "Unfortunately, it didn't get discovered until the suit was squashed. Billy Boyd was beyond furious when he didn't win the suit. The Jiltsons paid him what I suspect was a token amount to appease him, but I seriously doubted it would cool him down. He had to raise those five kids without their mother."

The chief, Celebrity and Jimmy stared at Betty as scenarios churned through their brains.

"Oh, wow," Jimmy said. "Where are those five Henderson kids now, do you know?"

"Two are still here in the area, one's dead, and the other two are in somewhere parts unknown to me," Betty said.

Chief Price nodded. "Okay, we've got something the Feds don't have. Let's keep this low-key so they don't botch up our investigation." He gave Jimmy the eye.

"I'll talk to Bill and Sylvan. We can develop this but not release anything until justice has been served, then the facts can come out," Jimmy said. He turned to his great-aunt. "How can I get a hold of that note?"

JIMMY AND BILL TRANCE were in a closed-door meeting in Sylvan's office. The suicide note couldn't have been more caustic, and Susan Henderson's words left them momentarily speechless.

Billy Boyd,

I've hated your guts for the past five years. All you think I'm capable of is to spit out babies and clean house. You've never let me follow my dream of going to school to become a teacher. All I do every day—day in and day out is watch the wallpaper grow old while listening to the kids screaming. You never lift a finger to help, and you don't act like a father. Well, you can do it all on your own because I'm not sticking around.

Sue

SYLVAN BROKE THE SILENCE. "That poor woman."

"You realize that she could have been leaving him, not committing suicide," Jimmy said.

Bill stared at Jimmy. "You think he murdered her?"

"It's not definitive. *I'm not sticking around* doesn't sound like someone who's going to off herself," Jimmy said. "I want to put a bug in the chief's ear."

"Okay, we've got a mystery to solve. Find out about that Henderson kid Betty said was dead. I want to know how and when he died. We're going to have to find out exactly what herbs were used in this apparent suicide. Need the coroner's report. I wonder if they did an autopsy forty years ago?" Sylvan was stirred by the note and what he considered weak circumstances all around.

"Susan would have been in her thirties when she died. Billy Boyd is still painting houses," Bill said. "He must be in his late seventies."

"I'll build a file," Jimmy said. "Do we have newspaper archives dating back forty years?"

"We invested in an online database. The library also has archives," Sylvan said.

Jimmy stood. "I'll start searching."

CHAPTER NINE

JIMMY DROVE BACK over to the police station. The chief was by himself, glaring at the screen. Jimmy tapped on the open doorframe.

"Got a minute? I want to run something by you."

"Help me fix this first. I've gotten rid of all unnecessary tabs, like you showed me, but I can't understand what's going on," Chief Price said.

Jimmy stood in back of his chair and looked over the chief's shoulder. "Click on the Styles Pane. I'll bet you set up a tab that's not showing up."

The chief did as Jimmy suggested, then looked under Format/Tabs in the current style. Sure enough, there was a wild tab setting.

"Hit that Clear All. Should remove that tab and reformat your document," Jimmy said.

"That did it. Okay, what did you want to run by me?" Chief Price asked.

"Have you studied that suicide note?" Jimmy asked.

"What about it?"

"That *I'm not sticking around* sounds more like Mrs. Henderson was packing her bags to leave Billy Boyd. Didn't sound like a suicide note to me," Jimmy said.

The chief sat up straighter, thinking about what Jimmy just said. "You're right. Could he have murdered his wife? How would he have gotten those herbs in her system, though? The herbs could not have been ingested after she died."

"You're right, but he could have held a gun to her head and forced her to take them." Jimmy nodded at his own hypothesis.

"Maybe she packed her bags and he found out about it." Chief Price nodded. "Have to dig into the files."

"I'm collecting data for a file," Jimmy said as he headed towards the door. "I'll be at the TIN if you need me."

Boller Henderson was seventeen when he was run down and killed by an unknown driver. Jimmy thought about that as he continued to read the archived article. He let his mind go with the flow. He wondered if perhaps Boller knew what had happened to his mother and was going to the cops. It was pure speculation on Jimmy's part, but he couldn't help but think about it. He wanted to find the two Hendersons who left town and never returned.

Jimmy hit up Google and entered Jeremy Henderson, Twinkle, TX. Dozens of listings came up for the name, but only two items surfaced related to Twinkle. He clicked on the first item. It was a piece in the TIN about Boller's funeral where Jeremy was mentioned. The second item was from five years ago. Jeremy Henderson got engaged to a woman in Boston.

Jimmy cross-checked and found addresses for both Jeremy and Helena Chatsworth in the Boston area. He thought about how to go about contacting Jeremy. What questions he should ask that wouldn't scare him off.

He knocked on Bill's open door, where he found the

managing editor gleefully circling bloopers in out-of-town newspapers with a red thin-tipped marker pen.

"Got a minute?" Jimmy asked.

"What'd you find out?" Bill asked.

"Were you aware that Boller Henderson was run down by a vehicle while riding his bike? He died at the scene."

"How old was he?" Bill was trying to place the news.

"Seventeen. Right about that time, his two older brothers left home," Jimmy said. "I located Jeremy in Boston. He got engaged five years ago. May already be married, but I didn't see any announcement."

"What about the other brother?" Bill asked.

"I haven't found Hunter yet. This is going to be delicate. How do I start a conversation with Jeremy where he doesn't cut me off? We need to find out if those kids will tell us anything we don't already know. I think Boller was killed intentionally. Maybe he was going to the cops."

Bill tapped his lips with the red marker, lost in thought about Jimmy's news, until he realized he was painting his lips red. He capped the marker, grabbed a napkin, dipped it in his cold coffee, and scrubbed his lips.

"JEREMY? MY NAME IS JIMMY KATZ." Jimmy kept his voice neutral. He had his phone's voice recorder enabled.

"Katz. You're that heir of Betty Diaz, aren't you? What are you calling me for?"

"Sounds like you're keeping somewhat up to date if you know that I'm Betty's heir," Jimmy said. "You've probably heard about the poisoning in Twinkle?"

"What's that got to do with me?" Jeremy asked.

"Nothing and everything," Jimmy said. "What happened when you were a little boy—how did your mother really die?"

There was silence on the line. For a minute, Jimmy thought the call had dropped, then he heard a distinct, long breath being released on the other end of the call.

"Mom was going to leave without us. We were little—I was seven at the time. Hunter was six, Boller was five, Joslin was three, and Marylou was a year and a half. My father found out and went berserk. He force-fed those drugs to her, and we watched her die. Boller's accident wasn't random. He was riding his bike to town to tell the police. Hunter and I tried to talk him out of it, but he just couldn't live with it anymore. He didn't make it to the police station. After his funeral, Hunter and I left Texas," Jeremy said.

"Do you still talk with your sisters? Could one of them, or your father, be responsible for this recent rash of poisonings in Twinkle?" Jimmy asked. He didn't think Jeremy would cut him off since he had supplied the facts.

"I honestly don't think they could be involved. Even dad. I don't know what there would be to gain now, after all these years," Jeremy said. "And Jiltson's had nothing to do with my mom's death, so this whole poisoning thing with that health food store doesn't sound like anything tied to my family."

"Keep my number handy in case you hear something I should check out," Jimmy said.

"I'd like to come home for a visit sometime, but there's way too much bad blood between me and my father. I don't think Helena would ever set foot in Twinkle, to tell the truth. She's a Boston girl and doesn't think much of small-town life," Jeremy said.

"I saw your engagement in the paper a few years ago. Did you get married?" Jimmy had a picture of a hoity-toity woman in his head.

"We're waiting for her to finish school. She's got her under-grad in business, but she's almost finished with her master's. Then we'll set a date," Jeremy said.

Jimmy didn't think it sounded very convincing. "I hope you decide to make a trip home. I'd be happy to meet with you."

"Thanks. I'll think about it. I'd better get going," Jeremy said.

They ended the call, and Jimmy sat in the conference room for a few minutes, digesting the conversation. Then he went in search of Bill Trance.

"I THINK you need to take that recording to Chief Price. Let him make a determination of how he wants to handle this information," Bill said.

Sylvan shook his head. "Those poor kids. The two girls most likely aren't affected by the murder of their mother because they were so little. But the boys! How could a father run down his own son? Someone explain it to me!"

"Sylvan, if he has no compunction about murdering his wife in front of his kids, killing one of them is just another day in a murderer's life," Bill said. "Jimmy, you go to the police station. I'll call the chief and tell him you're on the way."

Jimmy left, and Bill picked up the office phone. "Chief. Jimmy will be there in a few minutes. I think you'll want Detective Ramirez and Celebrity in on what he's going to tell you." They spoke for a few more minutes, then Bill heard Jimmy in the background.

CHIEF PRICE CALLED Ramirez and Celebrity into his office.

"Shut the door," he said.

Ramirez got up and closed the door. "What's going on?" He looked over to Jimmy, expecting to see a tell. He noticed he was mildly upset, but figured he'd wait until he heard what they were waiting to hear.

"I hunted down Jeremy Henderson and called him. I recorded the conversation, and you need to hear it." He pulled his phone out, pulled up his voice recorder and pressed Play.

When the recording ended, everyone started talking at once. Chief Price held up a hand. Celebrity was sniffing back tears.

"Jimmy, try to get ahold of Hunter and see if he will corroborate his brother's story. I'm leaning toward agreeing with Jeremy in that I don't see his family connected to the current poisonings. I don't see what they would benefit from them, and too much time has passed since Susan died," the chief said.

"Should we bring Billy Boyd in?" Ramirez asked.

"What we need is the death certificate and the autopsy report—we need to see how everything was determined forty years ago. The coroner could still be alive, and if he is, we need to question him about how Susan's death was handled," Chief Price said. "Tackle that, Ramirez."

"Joslin was three. She may have confused memories of what she saw," Celebrity said. "And, come to think of it, even though Marylou was only a year and a half, maybe Joslin talked to her sister about it, and when they were a little older, it could have been their big secret."

"I pulled up the voter registration website. Both of the girls are still in Starlight County. Joslin lives in Dime Water, and Marylou lives in Lockton. I don't want to stir up anything until we see what Jimmy gets from Hunter," the chief said.

"Celebrity, go talk to Bill Hill. See if he has any stories about the Henderson lawsuit, or anything else related to it."

The chief waited for his people to leave the office, then he eyeballed Jimmy. "You know we can't use that recording because it isn't legal."

Jimmy opened his mouth, but the chief cut him off.

"However, it will help when it comes time to get their statements. If Jeremy won't come to Twinkle, I can have the police in Boston take his statement so it will be official. We'll wait until we see what Hunter has to say."

"But it's better that I recorded the call, right?" Jimmy asked.

"Yes. We heard the story in Jeremy's own words. What those kids experienced could be considered child abuse today. To make them witness their mother's death, then to kill one of them?" Chief Price shook his head. "Why don't you give Hunter a call now? Ask him if you can record the conversation."

"Should I mention you're with me?"

"If he seems reluctant, I might chime in to change his mind. He could just hang up and refuse to cooperate, in which case I'll have him picked up and questioned," the chief said.

Jimmy took out his notepad and found Hunter Henderson's phone number, and placed the call. It was answered on the third ring.

Hello? Who is this?

"Hunter? This is Jimmy Katz."

There was silence on the line. Then, *my brother told me you called him, and that you'd be calling me.*

"Would it be okay if I recorded our conversation?"

I guess so. I'm ready to put this nightmare behind me. Please, just don't let my father know you located me. My sisters know where Jeremy and I live, but our father only knows we might be on the East Coast.

"Take me back to the day your mother died. Who was there? What did you see?" Jimmy asked.

We had just finished breakfast, so everyone was in the kitchen. Marylou was in her swing—one of those crank-up things. Joslin was at the table in her booster seat. Jeremy and I were in our places at the table. My mom and dad were yelling at each other. He had all these bottles on the table, and his handgun was in the waistband of his jeans.

"Do you know what type of gun it was, or if it was loaded?"

I don't know what kind of gun it was. It was most likely loaded because he used it or a rifle to shoot rats.

"The gun really isn't important because he didn't shoot anyone," Jimmy said. "What happened next?"

He opened the bottles and grabbed my mom's hair. He told her to eat the herbs. She didn't want to, so he held the gun to her head and started shoving these herbs in her mouth. Boller, Hunter, Joslin and I were screaming for him to let her go. We were all crying. He made her drink a glass of water, then her head hit the table and she shook all over. I know now that she was convulsing. Then she was dead.

Jimmy, and the chief heard the anxiety in Hunter's voice as he relived that day.

Dad told us that if we ever said one word about what happened, we'd end up like her. He wiped his prints off the jars, then held her hands to each of the jars to get her prints on the glass and the caps.

"What kind of jars were they?"

Those canning jars with the latching thing that closes them. You know what I mean?

"Yes. I've seen those jars at the store. Then what happened?"

He called the police and put on a believable act. They sent an ambulance. That was the last time we ever saw our mom.

"Was your mom leaving your father? Do you know if she had a suitcase packed?"

Yeah, she had it under their bed and he found it.

"What happened to Boller?"

Hunter's voice hitched.

He and Dad got in a fight. Boller was riding his bike to the police station, and Dad ran him down.

Hunter broke down and sobbed. *I hope you hang the son of a bitch. It won't bring my mother or my brother back, but justice will be done.*

"Hunter, do you think your father or sisters are involved with this poisoning in Twinkle?"

I don't really know. Jiltson paid my dad off to get rid of the lawsuit that the herbs killed our mother. I can't imagine what he would gain by poisoning a bunch of people.

"What about your sisters?"

They may be a little warped from what they experienced as young children, but if they were going to poison anyone, it would be our father, not total strangers.

Jimmy had a thought. "Do you know if your mother had a boyfriend? Maybe she was going to leave with someone?"

The chief nodded, his expression knowing.

I'm not sure. I sort of remember Mr. McMillan coming to the house several times when my father wasn't there.

"Who is Mr. McMillan? A neighbor?"

He lived down the street from us. We played with his kids sometimes.

The chief's fingers flew over the keyboard as he looked for the name in several places. He wrote one word on a piece of paper and held it up to Jimmy.

"Was it Douglas McMillan?"

Yeah, I'm positive Mom called him Doug.

"Hunter, I appreciate you talking to me. If you think of

anything else that would be helpful in bringing your father to justice, please call me or Chief Price."

I will. Too much time has passed. My father has had all these years. He needs to rot in prison.

The call ended, and Jimmy just stared at the chief for a long moment.

"Send me that voice recording. It's going to hang that bastard." Chief Price stood.

CHAPTER TEN

ERNIE STRUBHOLTER WORE thick magnifying goggles as he leaned over his table and studied dead bees. Entomology had always fascinated him, and when he retired from the coroner's office, he took it up as a hobby. A large, colorful poster hung on the wall of his office that celebrated World Bee Day on May 20th.

He noticed that one miner bee had a broken antenna. The fat, furry-looking yellow bee also had a broken wing. Miner bees (*Andrenidae*) made nests in the ground that had a narrow opening called a chimney. Ernie loved their chubby, bright appearance.

He stood and stretched just as his wife knocked on the doorframe.

"Ernie, you have a visitor," she said. "Someone from the police department."

"What do they want me for? They need to go see that feller who took my place." He replaced his goggles with his eyeglasses, muttering to himself as he followed his wife out of the room.

Detective Ramirez stood in the middle of the living room, waiting patiently. He mentally raised a brow as Ernie toddled into the room, his wife going in another direction.

"Dr. Strubholter? I'm police detective Benito Ramirez."

"Mister, not doctor," Ernie corrected. "Some medical examiners are not doctors or forensic pathologists."

"I stand corrected. Doctor Maxwell said I would be better off talking to you as he wasn't around forty years ago," Ramirez said.

"Forty years ago? What in the world are you digging into from back then?" Ernie asked.

"The Susan Henderson suicide," Ramirez said. "Chief Price would like to see the autopsy report and the death certificate."

Ernie stared at the detective. "Do you mean to tell me that Maxwell couldn't find the report, or didn't have the time to look for it?" He silently fumed over his successor's laziness. "Let's go then. Can you give me a ride back home?"

"Sure, no problem."

ERNIE AND RAMIREZ entered the building. The old medical examiner led the way to Dr. Maxwell's office.

"You couldn't find the file?" Ernie snipped to Maxwell.

Dr. Maxwell stood. "I figured it would be best to let you handle this."

Ernie harrumphed. "Come on, Ramirez. Your eyes are better than mine." He led the detective to a file storage room, turned on the bright lights, and stood inside the room. "Let's see. Look for case boxes from the 1980s."

Ramirez took one side of the room and began scanning the

dates on the shelves. He passed the 1950s, then the 1960s, and the 1970s. He found the 1980s. "Over here."

Ernie joined the detective. He pointed. "Grab that box. We'll start there."

Ramirez carried the box to a table in the middle of the room. Ernie opened the box and sifted through the case files. "Nope, put this box back and grab the next one."

Ernie found the Susan Henderson file in the third box. Both he and Ramirez studied the contents of the file. The original death certificate showed the cause of death as accidental poisoning from toxic herbs. Ernie sifted through the documents in the file until he found the autopsy report.

"There's no indication that this is a suicide. Looking at this report, there was a large amount of undigested toxic herbs in the stomach," Ernie stated. "Also, there were bruises on the deceased's body. See here, Ramirez? Face, arms, and collarbone had bruising. Very suspicious. Could have been murder."

"Can I get a copy of the file, or do we need to go through official channels?" Ramirez asked.

Ernie pointed to the printer.

"Think we can find the Boller Henderson file? Hit and run. He was 5 in 1982 when his mom died, so look for 1994. He would have been 17," Ramirez said.

RAMIREZ LED Ernie Strubholter through the police station to the chief's office. He tapped on the door frame. "Chief, this is Mr. Strubholter, the former medical examiner."

Chief Price stood and shook Ernie's hand. "What'd you find out?"

Ramirez handed over the copied file. "Looks like murder from the docs in the file."

"I'm not sure why anyone would have called this a suicide," Ernie said. "There's a clear indication of foul play just from reading the reports. How could this have been swept under the carpet?"

"Looks like we'll have to dig deeper. Find out who the DA was, Ramirez, and the Henderson's attorney as well," Chief Price said, as his eyes scanned the documents in the file. "Death certificate doesn't show suicide, so I'm not sure how that lawsuit with Trembo Jiltson even got off the ground. Very suspicious activity, all of this."

"I remember now. That Billy Boyd Henderson put up a ruckus about having to raise his five kids without a mother. Jiltson paid him fifty grand to make it go away," Ernie said.

"Boller died in 1994. The file shows he was killed by a hit-and-run vehicle while he was riding his bicycle. There was a paint scraping taken from his crumpled bike, but I didn't see anything in the file if it was compared with any known vehicles, such as Billy Boyd's vehicle," Ramirez said.

"Whatever vehicle he drove back then has most likely been scrapped by now—that was twenty-seven years ago, and who knows how many years Billy Boyd had the vehicle to begin with," Chief Price said.

Ernie now looked surprised. In his business, he had faced all sorts of nefarious situations. "Killed his own kid?" He shook his head. "Sometimes I wonder if the aliens ever did land here, if they had one good reason not to wipe man off the planet."

"We really appreciate your help," Chief Price said. "Please keep this to yourself. We don't want anything alerting Billy Boyd Henderson that we're opening up the cases."

"Happy to help. If you need me on the stand, I'm your guy. Let's put this man behind bars," Ernie said. He eyed Ramirez. "You taking me back home?"

CELEBRITY SAT across the kitchen table from Bill Hill in his house on Emerson Street, sipping iced tea. The kitchen cabinets were dark gray and the walls a pale gray. All the door and window frames were white, which brightened up the room.

Bill Hill looked worn out. His diamond earrings didn't seem to twinkle in the sunlight streaming through the window over the sink that held a couple of days-worth of dirty dishes. His Birkenstock sandals were tossed aside by the door to the garage, where he had stepped out of them the day the Feds told him to leave his store.

"I don't know who would want to do this to me," Bill said, his voice dragging with sadness.

Celebrity put on her cop voice to stir Bill out of his doldrums. "What do you know about the Susan Henderson suicide back in 1982?"

Bill stared at Celebrity for a moment. "1982? I was thirteen. I remember the scandal, but I don't know the details. Life was too busy with school, sports, girls—you know what I mean?"

"What about Boller Henderson? Do you remember him?"

"He was that kid who was killed by a hit and run when he was on his bike."

Celebrity watched him. "That's right."

Bill rubbed his mostly gray chin stubble. "I worked at a large health food store in Austin after I got my masters in 1992, and I didn't come back to Twinkle until 2000."

"Is that when you opened the Wellness Center?" Celebrity asked.

"Yeah. I saved as much of my earnings throughout college— you would not believe the dives I lived in! But I had this dream of having my own shop. And now look at it! What does this have to do with me?"

"We don't think it has anything to do with your store," Celebrity said.

"Then why did they take all of my inventory? Don't they have poison-sniffing dogs?" Bill's eyes implored her for answers.

Celebrity shook her head. "I don't know, Bill. Can you tell me how many of the products you sold were your own formulas?"

"Sure. Three. And these are my highest sellers! Wellness In A Bottle, Get It Up, and Thump, Thump, Thump."

"Tell me about the processing and packaging," Celebrity asked.

"Around eight years ago, I met with Trembo Jiltson about my Wellness In A Bottle. I had been making it myself for my own use all through college, and it really worked great. Anytime I felt like something was coming on, I'd take my formula and after only two or three doses, whatever was trying to hack into my immune system, let go and was gone." He smiled, recollecting the past. "After a lot of meetings with Trembo and our respective lawyers, we came to an agreement, and Jiltson became my manufacturer and packager."

"Does he sell your products through his clinic or his online store?" Celebrity asked.

"We have it worked out where we get percentages of online and in-store sales from each of our places," Bill explained. "Then I came up with the formulas for the other two products. I negotiated a better percentage for myself."

"My neighbor takes your Thump, Thump, Thump. She said it's saved her from having a stent," Celebrity said.

"Maybe when the Feds release my store and website, I can get a review from her," Bill said, without a lot of conviction. "I've got to tell you, my Get It Up formula practically flies off the shelves. I don't know what people are going to do now that they can't buy my products."

"It'll get better. We just have to chase as many leads as possible so we can catch whoever is doing this," Celebrity said as she stood.

RAMIREZ KNOCKED on the white door of the ranch-style house. The door opened and an older man with a clean-shaven face and dark brown hair with streaks of gray stood there.

"May I help you?" the guy asked.

"Are you Douglas McMillan?"

"Yes."

"I'm Detective Benito Ramirez, and I'd like to ask you some questions."

Douglas McMillan stared back with disbelieving eyes. "The police want to question me? About what? Did you catch me eating a grape I didn't pay for at the Foo and you're going to arrest me?"

Ramirez' lip curled up, trying not to smile. He thought he'd have a little fun with that confession. "You do realize that people who picked their noses, scratched their butts, cleaned their ears with their fingers—they had their fingers all over those grapes."

Mr. McMillan's eyes went into headlight mode as he realized the error of his ways. "Geez."

"May I come in, or do you want to step outside?" Ramirez said. He wanted to get down to business.

"Oh! Sure, please come in!" Mr. McMillan opened the door wide and stepped out of the way. He showed Ramirez to the sofa in the living room. "Please make yourself comfortable."

Ramirez sat on the sofa and waited for Douglas McMillan to sit.

"So, what is this about?" Mr. McMillan asked.

"We're looking into Susan Henderson's death back in 1982," Ramirez stated. He closely watched Douglas McMillan's face for any signs of discomfort. He noticed a tiny flinch. "What was your relationship with her around that time?"

Mr. McMillan lowered his eyes to the carpet as a sadness swept over him. He looked up and met Ramirez' eyes. "I was going to leave my wife, and she was going to leave Billy Boyd."

"Did she plan to leave her children behind?" Ramirez didn't have any sympathy for the man. Leaving those kids with Billy Boyd was reprehensible.

"We'd never leave them with that monster. Sue and I planned to get everyone in the car as if I were taking them to school, then never come back."

"What happened?"

"I don't know how he found out. We never told the kids, but he must have suspected she was going to leave him. The next thing I knew, she was dead." He unashamedly sobbed into his hands. "After her funeral, Boller told me he was scared that his dad would make them eat herbs and kill them too."

"You didn't go to the police?" Ramirez asked.

"Billy Boyd's second cousin was the DA. I didn't think there would be a chance to talk to anyone who could take any action," Mr. McMillan said. "Everyone knew that Dude Richards was rotten to the core. He and Billy Boyd were closer than cousins. They shared that complete rottenness." He shook his head. "For the life of me, I didn't understand why Sue married him. She said that he wasn't like that in their early time together."

"Dude?" Ramirez asked.

"That's his first name."

"What about your wife and kids?" Ramirez asked. "You were just going to walk out on them?"

"My wife's family would have taken care of them. I know that sounds terrible, but my wife had certain expectations, and when I didn't live up to them, things soured between us."

"Are you still married to her?"

"No, she left about fifteen years ago. Married a rich fella from Austin," Mr. McMillan said.

"Do you think it's possible that Billy Boyd or any of the kids would be involved in these latest poisonings?" Ramirez asked.

Douglas McMillan acted as if Ramirez had slapped him. "You can't be serious! What would be the point?"

"Why did you stay here after your wife left?" Ramirez asked.

"I wanted to make sure the Henderson kids had someone to talk to if they ever needed to. It was a very terrible time for those kids, especially when Boller was killed. Jeremy and Hunter left with the clothes on their backs and whatever they could stuff into their backpacks. I gave them bus money and helped when I could," he said.

JIMMY, Celebrity, and Ramirez sat in front of the chief's desk. They each had outlined their investigation conclusions, which brought them back to a complete lack of any suspect.

"We're definitely missing something significant," the chief said.

"Maybe this poisoning doesn't have anything to do with the Hendersons?" Jimmy asked.

Ramirez, Celebrity and the chief acknowledged him with a nod.

"Ramirez, hunt down Dude Richards. Could be dead by

now. Find his cases from 1982 to 1994. Let's see if he withheld evidence," Chief Price said.

CHAPTER ELEVEN

Jimmy sat at his desk at the boarding house typing at Mach speed as if he were in a competition. Maddy watched his hands fly over the keyboard from where she perched on his desk. She reached out a paw, but withdrew it. Jimmy was determined to capture all the details that he, Ramirez and Celebrity has sniffed out before they became weak memories. This included the devastating lives the Henderson kids, and even Doug McMillan waded through all those years. He shook his head as scenarios flooded his mind.

It brought back sad memories of when he discovered that his parents hadn't died in a regular car accident, but were murdered through the deranged librarian's scheme which caused an intentional malfunction of their vehicle.

"Maddy, you would not believe what these people have had to live with," Jimmy said.

His kitten made a noise that he swore sounded like, *yeah*.

Guppy monitored the outdoor activity through his two windows. He scooted across the branches on his fake tree, taking in the trees, the backyard, and the road. "Cops!" He belted out.

A few minutes later, the downstairs door was answered by his landlady, and he heard someone climbing the stairs. He beat them to the door and opened it to Celebrity.

"Hey," he said.

"Hi," she said. "Can we talk?"

"As long as it isn't about Tulip and Dorchester," Jimmy said, dead serious.

"Honestly, I'll never live that down!" she huffed out, as Maddy wrapped herself around Celebrity's feet.

"Come on in. I was just finishing up my notes from the meeting this morning," he said as he stood aside to let her into the apartment.

Celebrity stepped around a darting Maddy and walked over to Jimmy's desk.

"That's what I wanted to talk about. How do you think this will play out? If that DA from forty years ago, and maybe the former police chief were dirty, will Norbert Rosas do anything about it?"

Jimmy thought about the current DA. He had dealings with Rosas when Divinia Reynolds, the former head librarian, was arrested and tried. "I don't think he will brush anything aside. If anything, I think he'll latch onto what we dug up and will swiftly seek justice that's long overdue."

"I hope so. Poor Bill Hill! His livelihood was swept away in a single stroke. And those Henderson kids!" Celebrity said.

"Don't forget Doug McMillan. They're all crushing experiences," Jimmy said.

"We're back to square one with the current situation," Celebrity said. "It seems to me that the Feds don't have a clue, because surely we'd see some activity."

"Maybe we're not on the right trail," Jimmy said. "I can't

seem to find any other connection to these poisonings. I'm just glad it has nothing to do with me this time!"

"If we could only figure out who would gain by these poisonings. I'm not even sure how to determine what would be gained, except for abnormal satisfaction that people are suffering," Celebrity stated.

"I bet everyone who brought their bottles to the police station will want a refund," Jimmy said. "They won't be able to process one online with the website shut down. I wonder how that will play out when things are back to normal."

"Normal... that would be so nice. I'm looking forward to a low-key time where I'm chasing down someone who ran a stop sign, or dealing with kids smoking behind the bleachers. But I've got to tell you, Jimmy, I will scrutinize any domestic abuse calls to make sure there are no *Hendersons* on my watch."

Jimmy pulled her to him, wrapped his arms around her, and kissed her thoroughly.

DETECTIVE RAMIREZ SAT at his desk and mulled over all the pieces of the poisoning case that the team had pulled together so far. After discovering the death certificate and autopsy report from Susan Henderson's demise, Ernie Strubholter adamantly stated that there was no way that her death could be construed as a suicide. Ramirez didn't like where that clearly led.

Big City cops, attorneys, and district attorneys were a mix of clean and dirty. But cops and law enforcement officials in Twinkle, Texas, a small town of three thousand? He refused to think that Dude Richards was that rotten. Then there was the police chief from forty years ago.

Ramirez woke his computer by jiggling his mouse. He

couldn't use a touchpad to save his life, so had bought a mouse. Benito signed into his account with the strong password that was required for all law enforcement personnel, and searched for a database that listed the who's who of Twinkle history, which would include ones from forty years ago.

He found police chief Terrance Love in the database, but he had retired three years prior to the Henderson case. Gordon Muller was voted into office in 1982. Ramsey Kent had been the acting chief between the two. Ramirez searched for their personnel files and printed them. He wanted to hold pages in his hands and use an actual highlighter when necessary. For some odd reason, he thought better with something he could touch.

The detective walked over to the shared printer and gathered the pages, then returned to his desk. He set Gordon Muller's pages aside, wanting to concentrate on Ramsey Kent. He had a moment, then pulled up an external link to the internet. Ramirez keyed in *Ramsey Kent, Twinkle, TX*, then hit the return key. A genealogy site popped up that law enforcement officials used periodically. He hunted through his desk to find the login information.

Irritated that he had to retype the name, Ramirez finally discovered the correct family tree. He plowed through the family structure until he hit the jackpot that he knew in his gut he would find.

Billy Boyd Henderson was indeed second cousin to Dude Richards. And, lo-and-behold, Ramsey Kent was related to Dude. That was how the murder of Susan Henderson was switched to a suicide, and how Billy Boyd got away with murdering his own son. Ramirez printed out the two pages that revealed the family connections, grabbed the pages and headed to Chief Price's office.

When he found the office empty, he backtracked to the small kitchen where the coffee, drink and snack machines were located, but the chief wasn't there. He headed up front to where Sgt. Gonzales was stationed.

"Did the chief go somewhere?"

"Yeah, left about ten minutes ago," Sgt. Gonzales said.

"Know where he went?" Ramirez asked.

"Nope."

"How about Celebrity? Know where she is?" Ramirez asked.

"Nope. I'm not in their confidence, but I can radio them for their 10-20," Sgt. Gonzales said, being a smart Alec.

Ramirez gave him the stink eye. "That's why you're still at this desk after four years." He huffed back to his desk.

Detective Ramirez returned his search to the personnel files and found what he was looking for. He pulled out his cellphone and called the chief.

The chief answered on the second ring. "What's up?"

"I know how the Henderson murders were swept under the carpet," Ramirez said.

"Drive over to the boarding house," Chief Price said.

Ramirez grabbed all his paperwork and slid it inside a clasp envelope and headed out. He saw that both the chief and Celebrity were at the boarding house when he turned the corner onto Burbridge Street. He pulled up in back of the deputy's cruiser and headed for the door.

Mrs. Potts opened the door. "Well, it looks like the entire police force is here. Go on up to Jimmy's place."

"Thanks, Mrs. Potts."

He took the stairs two at a time and rapped on the door. The chief answered the door. "Come on in. We're having an impromptu meeting. Show us what you've got."

"Cops!" Guppy squawked out.

Celebrity held a sprawled, sleeping cat in her arms.

Ramirez walked over to the kitchen table and pulled the paperwork out of the envelope. "One mystery solved. Wish it was the problem with this poisoning, but at least we can put the Henderson murders to rest."

They all huddled around the kitchen table as Ramirez laid it all out, pointing from one document to the other. "According to their personnel records for retirement benefits, Richards and Kent are still alive."

"We are going to tank them," Chief Price said. "They can spend their golden years under lock and key. Never in my wildest thoughts would I have suspected that Twinkle held such devious law enforcement people. Ramirez, I want you and Celebrity to pull together an obvious scenario with documentation that can't be refuted. We need to have everything sewn tightly to bring this to Rosas. I want arrests and convictions. Understand?"

"With pleasure," Ramirez said.

"I look forward to handcuffing Billy Boyd Henderson," Celebrity said.

"Hopefully, once this is out of the way, we can get to the bottom of these poisonings," Jimmy said.

MRS. POTTS CHOPPED ONIONS, carrots, and celery. She added them to the stewpot, where a nice roast had been braised on all sides. She filled an empty pitcher with water and added it to the pot, then added half a pitcher more. After cleaning up the kitchen, she hauled out the vacuum to tackle the hall and entryway. Next up, she grabbed her cleaning tote and headed for the half bath.

After that chore, she returned to the kitchen and checked on the stewpot to find it nicely bubbling. She added salt, pepper, thyme, basil, and garlic powder. Humming a little tune, she grabbed her tote and headed to Brian's bathroom to give it a good scrub. The journalist tried hard to keep his apartment clean, but it was impossible to live up to his landlady's standards.

Mrs. Potts finished Brian's bathroom and climbed the stairs to Jimmy's place. Everyone had cleared out an hour ago, so she opened the door and greeted the animals.

"Guppy, are you being a good bird?"

"Angel!" the parrot squawked.

"I seriously doubt that," Mrs. Potts said. She looked around and found Maddy buried in the sofa cushions. "Well, don't you look comfy." She headed to Jimmy's bathroom and gave it a scrub, then went back downstairs, leaving the door open. She loved it when the animals came to visit her.

Mrs. Potts shelved the cleaning tote in the pantry, where a cleaning closet separated chemicals from food products. Then she got out a soup spoon and tasted the simmering broth, then rinsed the spoon and set it on the small salad plate she used as a spoon rest.

"Oh, that's good." She took the big slotted spoon and gave the ingredients a stir. She liked to simmer her stews and meats for at least four to six hours before adding in chunks of potatoes.

Mrs. Potts sampled the broth again—she dipped a scoop into the pot and filled a small bowl with around a quarter of a cup of broth. She blew on the hot liquid, shook the salt shaker into the bowl, then slurped it down, smacking her lips and letting out a satisfied *ah*.

Maddy and Guppy made their appearance in the kitchen.

Guppy took up residence on his favorite chair-back, and Maddy batted a bottle cap across the floor.

"Mrs. Potts will give you a snack in a little while," she told them. She sat at the table and picked up her mystery novel to delve back into the story on page seventy-five. After a few minutes of reading, she set the book down. "Oh, I don't feel so good."

Then her head crashed onto the table.

Maddy stopped what she was doing and jumped onto the table. She nudged the landlady. She sniffed at her beloved person.

Pots sick! Maddy told Guppy.

"Pots!" the parrot belted out.

Maddy took off up the stairs and jumped onto Jimmy's desk. She batted the mouse to wake the computer. Then she grabbed her yellow pencil with the bite marks and gripped it firmly between her jaws. She gave the green message icon a good whack and stared at the screen. She recognized Jimmy's name, then started whacking keys.

JIMMY PULLED his car into the curved driveway of the mansion when his phone announced an incoming text. It was the distinctive tone he had set up for Home, which meant it was from Maddy. He grabbed his phone and read the text.

POTS! HELP!

"Oh, no!" He rammed his foot on the gas pedal and sped out of the driveway and onto Diaz Circle. Then he punched in speed dial #2 for Chief Price.

The chief answered in his semi-professional voice when he saw it was the heir calling. "Price."

"Maddy sent a text! Something's happened to Mrs. Potts!"

"I'm on the way!" The chief said. When the cat made contact, it was an emergency. He rushed to Stephanie's cubicle. "Send an ambulance to Mrs. Potts' place!" Then he was out the door.

Jimmy's car screeched to a halt in front of the boarding house. He was out the door and onto the porch as the chief's cruiser screeched around the corner and plowed over the curb and onto the lawn. He raced to the porch as Jimmy unlocked the door.

They both rushed to the most obvious place: the kitchen.

Maddy meowed in distress as she paced the table where Mrs. Potts hadn't moved.

"Pots!" Guppy hollered as he rocked sideways on the chair back.

"I've called an ambulance," Chief Price told Jimmy.

Jimmy rushed to his landlady and checked for a pulse. He was relieved when he found one. He and the chief studied her face. There wasn't any foaming at the mouth, which was the first thing they considered.

"Turn off the stove," Chief Price said.

They heard the ambulance arrive as Jimmy shut off the gas to the burner. He went to the door and held it open, waiting for the EMTs to gather their equipment.

"Down the hall to the kitchen," he directed.

Jimmy and the chief stood aside and watched the EMTs. One of them gave a cursory check of Mrs. Potts' vitals, then they moved her from the chair to the floor. That's when they noticed a slight bubbling in her mouth.

"Poison!" the lead EMT said.

"Oh, no!" Jimmy wailed.

The front door slammed open and Brian rushed into the

kitchen, clearly in a panic, which escalated when he saw Mrs. Potts on the floor. "What happened?"

Chief Price studied the entire scene. The pot on the stove, the little sample bowl, the spoons. He pulled out his phone and made a call. "Agent Wilson? Chief Price. We have a much bigger problem."

CHAPTER TWELVE

LUCKILY, all the ingredients for the stewpot were still on the counter: a bag of onions, carrots, celery, the spice jars, the water pitcher, and the unopened sack of potatoes.

Agent Wilson and the Feds swarmed the place. Jimmy had to secure his animals in his apartment. It had been a challenge to keep Maddy off the gurney that hauled their beloved landlady out of the boarding house.

Brian rushed into the kitchen. "Mrs. Potts cleaned my bathroom. Do you think it could have been poison in the cleaning supplies?"

"Where does she keep those?" Agent Wilson asked.

Jimmy jumped into action. "In the cleaning closet in the pantry!"

Wilson stopped him, holding up his hand in a *stop* motion. "I need everyone to clear out of here."

"Out of the kitchen, or out of the entire boarding house? I have two animals upstairs!" Jimmy balked loudly.

"This entire building is a crime scene. Pack up provisions and leave," Wilson said.

"For how long?" Brian barked back.

Agent Wilson didn't come across as acidic as he typically would, but he wasn't friendly by any means. "It could be awhile."

Jimmy opened his mouth, but Chief Price headed him off. "Okay. Understood." He turned to Brian and Jimmy. "Pack what you need. It could be several weeks."

Jimmy pulled his phone out. "Aunt Betty? There's been a terrible tragedy. Mrs. Potts has been poisoned. She's on the way to the hospital. The Feds told us to get out. Brian and I need a place to stay, along with my kitten and bird." He listened, calmed. "Okay. We'll be there soon."

Brian nodded and took off for his apartment.

Jimmy took to the stairs, followed by Chief Price. Clearly in a panic, Jimmy looked around. Then he looked up. "Should I remove the cameras?" he whispered to the chief.

"Do you have a screwdriver?" the chief asked.

"There's a tool bag in the hall closet downstairs." Jimmy said.

"You gather your stuff and I'll take care of this." Chief Price was out the door and down the stairs.

"Okay, we're going to camp out at Aunt Betty's house. Won't that be fun? You'll go for a ride in the car again."

"CAR!" Guppy belted out.

Maddy looked worried.

"Don't worry, Maddy. You'll love Aunt Betty's place. It's a big mansion with a lot of places to explore."

He shut down and unplugged his laptop. He grabbed the case from under the desk and loaded the laptop, the mouse, cords, Maddy's pencil, his phone charger, and everything else that would fit inside, then zipped it and set it beside the door. Then he headed to his bedroom. Jimmy pulled out his rolling suitcase, set it on the bed, and unzipped it. He methodically opened dresser drawers and stacked underwear, T-shirts, shorts, jeans, socks, and the folded long-sleeved dress shirts from the laundry.

He stuffed his sandals and tennis shoes with the soles facing away from the clean clothes. Jimmy grabbed his alarm clock and found a place for it in the suitcase. Next, he unzipped the suit bag and studied his hanging clothes. He grabbed what he thought he might need and zipped the bag. Jimmy was almost out the door when he remembered his bathroom necessities. He made sure all bottles were shut tight, then thought better about putting anything into his toiletries kit.

Jimmy raced to the kitchen. The chief was standing on a chair, unscrewing a camera.

"Almost finished," Chief Price said.

Jimmy went to his pantry and grabbed the box of gallon-sized zip bags, then returned to the bathroom. He stuffed his bottles of liquid soap and shampoo into a gallon bag, sealed it, then placed it in his kit. When he had all his shaving supplies and everything else bagged up, he hauled things out to the front door.

He scooped Maddy's litter box and disposed of her potty down the toilet. Then he carefully stuck the bag of litter in the box, along with the scooper, and added it to the pile by the door. He bagged up cat food and Guppy's bird seed. Then he opened the refrigerator and pulled out Guppy's food bins.

"I'm going to bring these things out to my car, then I've got to disassemble Guppy's tree."

Chief Price stepped down from the chair. "Got a bag I can put these in?"

"Pantry," Jimmy said. He grabbed the easiest things, his suitcase and briefcase, headed out the door and down the stairs. As he opened the front door, the limo pulled up with Toombs behind the wheel. He popped the trunk, then stepped out of the car.

Toombs called out. "Where's everything you're bringing?"

"Upstairs, right inside the door. I have to cage up my bird and take apart his fake tree."

Toombs headed to the house while Jimmy went around the limo to the opposite side and opened one of the rear doors. He deposited his luggage and briefcase on the floor. He figured he'd save the trunk for the litter box and everything to do with his pets.

Jimmy headed to the house and passed Toombs and the chief.

"Put everything for the animals in the trunk."

Jimmy hurried to the fake tree where Guppy nervously paced. "Don't worry, it's going to be okay. Come on, I need to put you in your travel cage, okay?"

He held out his arm and transferred his parrot to the sleep travel cage. He unhooked the cage from the stand and carried both to the door and set them down.

Jimmy looked around and thought about how he would transport Maddy. He didn't have a box or a travel cage for her. He went to the pantry and snagged her gazebo basket.

"Maddy? Come get in the basket so you can ride over to Aunt Betty's house."

His kitten rushed over to the basket and hopped inside as if she was afraid of being left behind. Jimmy grabbed her cushion and flung it over toward the door, then crawled around to gather her favorite toys and added those to the basket.

Toombs stomped up the stairs. "The chief had to go. I'll grab the rest of these things."

"Okay, thanks for your help." He turned to Maddy. "Stay in the basket while Daddy takes apart Guppy's tree, okay?"

Maddy hunkered down in the basket.

Jimmy removed the stainless steel bowls from the holders on the tree and set them by the door. Then he grabbed the tools and tackled the fake tree. He eyed it and determined he only had to remove the two branches. He was positive he could slip the whole thing into the deep trunk of the limo with those branches removed.

Toombs returned to the apartment and joined Jimmy by the tree. "That should fit in the trunk now."

"I thought so." Jimmy put the tools away.

He grabbed the trunk of the tree and Toombs grabbed the two branches. They stomped down the stairs and out of the house to the limo. Guppy's tree was eased into the trunk and the lid closed.

They returned to the house and climbed the stairs. Guppy waited patiently in his cage, and Maddy sat in her basket. Jimmy walked through the living room, trying to determine if he was leaving anything important behind. Then he looked around the kitchen and his desk.

"I hope I have everything important," he said. "Can you grab the birdcage?"

Toombs grabbed the cage and Jimmy picked up Maddy's basket. They left the apartment.

"Should I lock my door?"

"I would. They didn't say anything about needing access to your place, did they?" Toombs asked.

"No, the kitchen was the crime scene. He said Brian and I should gather our stuff and leave," Jimmy said.

"Let's go then," Toombs said.

JENKINS LENT A HAND unloading the limo to the large suite on the second floor of the mansion. Brian helped with the last of Jimmy's possessions. Between the four of them, the animals and all that was hauled into the suite was being set up. Jenkins took over Jimmy's clothing while Toombs tackled Guppy's fake tree.

When the tree was together in a corner with two window views, the bowls installed with food and water, and newspaper on the floor, Jimmy took in their temporary living quarters. No kitchen.

"I'm going to have to get a refrigerator," he said.

His Aunt Betty appeared in the doorway to the suite. She shouted to her assistant. "Elnora, order a refrigerator for Jimmy's suite."

Elnora came to the bottom of the stairs. "Medium sized? Not like the one in the kitchen, right?"

"Medium should do. Have it delivered today," Betty hollered back.

"Gotcha," Elnora said.

"Jimmy, take those down to the kitchen until your refrigerator arrives," Betty said.

"Thanks, Aunt Betty. I want to get to the hospital. Mrs. Potts..." he couldn't finish what he was saying.

"We can only pray that she pulls through," Betty said. "There's going to be panic in the community with this new scenario. The Feds need to let us know what was poisoned and where it came from."

When everyone left his suite, Jimmy closed the door and sat on the sofa. Maddy climbed onto his lap while Guppy checked out the new views.

"You two get to know our new place," he said, talking in a soothing voice. "We're going to have to live here for a while until the Feds let us go back home."

"FEDS!" Guppy belted out.

"Why don't you watch TV, or explore our temporary

home while I go to the hospital and visit Mrs. Potts," Jimmy said. He picked up the remote and turned on the humongous TV that hung on the wall. "Keep the noise down, okay?" He placed the remote beside Maddy's cushion.

A rap sounded on the door. Maddy dashed off ahead of Jimmy. He opened the door to Brian.

"Want me to take you back to the house to get your car?" Brian asked.

"Oh! Hadn't even thought about it in all the confusion. Want to go to the hospital and check on Mrs. Potts?" Jimmy asked.

"Yeah, we'll go there first, then get your car."

Jimmy stooped to pet Maddy.

"Guppy, be a good boy," he called out from the door.

"Good boy," the bird squawked, as he monitored the outdoors through his windows.

Jimmy and Brian left the place.

"Where's your place?" Jimmy asked.

Brian pointed. "Third door down on the left."

They went down the stairs.

"Better tell my aunt where we're going," Jimmy said.

He led them toward her office, where they found her clacking away on her keyboard like a speed demon.

"I bet you won typing contests!" Brian said.

Betty looked up while continuing to type. "Ha! Those old manual typewriters were a challenge. You really had to pound the keys and hit the return arm. People got spoiled when the electric typewriter came out."

"We're going to the hospital, then Brian's going to take me back to the boarding house to get my car," Jimmy said.

"Ask Dr. Canada to give me a full report," Betty said.

"Will do. Thanks for putting us up," Jimmy said. "If it

weren't for you being here, I don't know where we would have gone."

"You can stay as long as you like," Betty said.

JIMMY AND BRIAN stood quietly outside the ICU room and looked through the glass. Mrs. Potts was hooked up to monitoring equipment and appeared to be sleeping.

"Should we go into the room?" Brian asked.

"Not sure," Jimmy said.

A moment later, their landlady's eyes fluttered open and wandered to the big window. She smiled weakly and wiggled fingers into a tiny wave.

Brian grabbed the door handle and he and Jimmy went inside.

"Hi, Mrs. Potts," Jimmy said, keeping his voice quiet.

She looked from Jimmy to Brian. "What happened? I hope someone turned off the stove."

"You were poisoned!" Brian spit out.

Mrs. Potts looked incredulously at her boarder. "What? How?"

They leaned in closer.

"Maddy sent me a text saying you needed help," Jimmy whispered.

"The EMTs determined it was poison, and Chief Price called Agent Wilson," Brian whispered.

Mrs. Potts' eyes tracked from one boarder to the next. "What was poisoned? I was cooking a pot roast."

"We don't know yet," Jimmy said. "They made us gather our stuff and told us to leave, so we're staying over at Aunt Betty's for now."

"Oh, no. I won't be able to go home when I'm discharged from the hospital?"

"Doesn't look like it," Brian said.

The door opened, and Agent Wilson entered the room. "I was notified that you were awake, Mrs. Potts." He eyed Jimmy and Brian.

"We'd better go now so you can talk to the FBI," Jimmy said. "We'll see you later."

Brian and Jimmy slinked out of the ICU room. They looked through the large window, but Agent Wilson glared at them, so they took off.

"Mrs. Potts, I'm Agent Wilson with the FBI. Chief Price contacted me when it was determined that you were poisoned. We're processing everything from your kitchen counter, the contents of the stewpot, the items on the kitchen table, and the cleaning supplies to determine which of the items contained the poison."

Mrs. Potts stared at Agent Wilson, trying to make sense of what he had said.

"Can you tell me if any of those items were purchased this week, and where?" Agent Wilson asked.

Her eyes rolled around, taking in the room while she thought things through. "I bought a new box of salt, all the produce, the roast, and toilet cleaner yesterday from the Foo— that's the Dime Water Food store. The light on the 'd' burned out a decade ago, and everyone calls it the Foo."

"Is the Dime Water Food store the only grocery store in the area?" Agent Wilson asked.

"Yes. People from all around the county shop there." She thought for a moment. "I think I bought the paperback yesterday, but I can't remember."

"Starlight County includes the towns of Twinkle, Star,

Clem's Corner, Bridge, Dime Water, Jupiter, Lockton, Pancake, and Derrick?"

"Yes. They're all small towns, with Twinkle being the largest," Mrs. Potts said. "Will I be able to go home when the hospital releases me?"

Agent Wilson shook his head. "Not until we know for sure what was used to transmit the poison. Then, after we have a solid source, you will have to have a hazmat team clean your interior; otherwise, you could unintentionally poison yourself again."

Her eyes were wide as she understood the severity of the situation. "Oh, my."

CHAPTER THIRTEEN

The Dime Water Foo(d) store was the only supermarket that provided for the towns in the county, with hours from six in the morning until midnight. Small convenience stores and several ice houses dotted the towns, but for the long haul of weekly, or holiday shopping, the Foo was it in Starlight County.

A growing crowd stood outside the locked doors of the Foo that sported a huge sign in English, Spanish, Chinese, and Hindi:

TEMPORARILY CLOSED

No other explanation, but all anyone had to do was look around and see the different government vehicles, and watch the activity of federal agents inside.

"Look, they've got dogs in there!" a man said.

"There must be tainted food in there. I heard on the police scanner that Bertha Potts was taken to the hospital yesterday, and there's crime scene tape on her front door," someone else said.

"Where are we supposed to go grocery shopping?"

"The closest store like the Foo is in Everston."

"Everston is 125 miles away!"

"Hey, look. Someone's coming to the door!"

The crowd watched as a black-suited man taped another sign on the door:

IF YOU PURCHASED ANYTHING FROM THE BAKING AND SPICE AISLE THIS WEEK, BRING THOSE ITEMS TO THE POLICE STATION IMMEDIATELY.

Danny Stonerich snapped pictures with his phone. He got a picture of one dog and its handler, the sign just posted to the door, and he had recorded conversations of the crowd.

As he left the storefront, he called his father. "Hey Dad, I've got the scoop on the Foo."

Sylvan, in turn, called Betty and relayed the information.

The Starlight County matriarch made one phone call that would gather the volunteers over at the Stardust Ballroom at the edge of Twinkle. It had been several years, if not more than a decade, since caravans headed out to outlying cities in an emergency run for food and provisions. It wasn't easy stocking for the 17,500 residents of Starlight County. Her team would call those stores and alert the managers as to when they would be on the way. Every available large truck, and four refrigerated trucks that would haul perishables, was called into service.

They prepared the grocery lists according to an aisle-by-aisle layout most common in supermarkets.

When Jimmy and Brian drove up the curved driveway, Toombs was waiting beside the town car with the engine running.

"What's going on?" Jimmy asked his shooting mentor.

"Emergency situation with the Foo shutting down. Betty's called in the volunteers," Toombs said.

Betty came out of the mansion. "Get in the car, or follow."

"Where are we going?" Brian asked.

"To the Stardust Ballroom," Betty said, as she slid onto the seat where Toombs held the door open.

"Where is that? I've never heard of it," Jimmy said. "I've got to feed my animals first."

"It's on the outskirts of town heading toward Clem's Corner," Toombs said.

"Okay, I'll see you there when I finish," Jimmy said.

Brian slid into the back seat of the town car, and Toombs took off.

JIMMY KEPT MUTTERING to himself as he passed each mile marker. He was about ready to pull over to the side of the road to call Toombs when suddenly a huge sign beside a triple-wide driveway appeared around the next bend.

The Starlight Ballroom was gigantic. The parking lot was packed. He found a place to park on the back forty and trotted to the entrance. When he opened the door, he was slammed with the cacophony of voices from groups of people sitting at round tables. He took in the organized chaos and found his aunt standing in the center of things, so he headed that way.

"What can I do to help?" he shouted near her ear.

"The grocery store managers are waiting on our lists so their warehouses can pull stock and have it ready for us at the stores," she said in a raised voice. "Go over there and look for Irma Sue Delaney, who's standing in for Mrs. Potts."

"I've never met her..."

"Look for a lady wearing a bright blue dress." Betty nudged him in the right direction.

Jimmy eased through the crowd and found Irma. "My aunt said to come help you."

"Oh, hello Jimmy. I'm trying to fill Mrs. Potts' shoes. Call me Irma Sue," she said.

"What's your group supposed to do?" he asked.

"We have extensive grocery lists that are divided into sixty groups in the room. Our group has aisle 14, which contains the vitamins, nutrition, allergy remedy's, eye care, and a lot of other things. What we need to do is to make sure the list is as complete as possible so the correct items can be pulled," Irma Sue explained.

"Wow, that's incredible."

"A long time ago, we all swarmed the stores with our lists, but all that changed. Now, we send the lists to the store managers, and they pull stock from the back, or have the ware-house send it to the store for us to pick up," she said.

"So, are we proofing the list against a store?" he asked.

"In a way. We're comparing our lists to the lists from the four stores that can accommodate us," Irma Sue said.

"Oh. As long as we have the master lists, this should be relatively easy," Jimmy said.

Irma Sue smiled.

An hour later, Jimmy was still at a laptop updating the massive master list for the second store. Two more stores to go. There were thousands of items on aisle fourteen. Who knew how many types of antacids there were? Or laxatives? The vitamin and supplement lists went on forever. He had two people helping him.

The other three people had their hands full with their mini-groups, correcting their items against the store's current stocking scheme.

Another hour into the process, the front doors opened, and the area restaurants brought in trays of food to feed the volunteers. It was a community-wide emergency, and everyone pitched in.

At one point, Jimmy spotted Brian. He thought he saw Danny, but there were so many people it was hard to tell. He was shocked to see Gigi Thompson, the staff writer who went off the rails several months back and had to give up her job to recover. There was no mistaking her natural blonde hair and her almost white eyebrows.

He stayed with his group so he wouldn't get lost. Their table held a small stand with the number fourteen on it, and he soon realized that tables were called up to the food line according to the aisle number they were working. He was glad he wasn't at table 50, but noticed the efficiency in the food serving line.

Things quieted down a decibel or two when people started to eat. They had a choice between sandwiches, spaghetti, and salads served on paper plates. Vats of iced tea were set up, and party-sized coffee makers brewed coffee.

Betty stood with a handheld microphone in the center of the room. "Hello? May I have your attention, please?" A hush swept over the room. "A lot of you are new to this process, and it has been quite a long time for the regular volunteers, so I thought I'd better let you know how this works. After we have our master lists ready for the store managers, they will be scanned and emailed to the stores. The next step is setting up the ballroom for the delivery of the merchandise. That includes getting the shelving, refrigerated containers, and freezers out of the warehouse and setting them up here."

"Are we doing that tomorrow morning?" someone yelled out.

"Yes. All volunteers will meet here tomorrow morning.

While we wait for the store managers to contact us and let us know everything is ready for pickup, we will set up the ballroom like a grocery store. Bertha Potts was the one who came up with this clever idea, but unfortunately, she's in the hospital recovering from being poisoned."

JIMMY WOKE bleary-eyed from interrupted sleep. He tried to shake off the mental recital and typing from the lists, but figured it might take a while. When he stumbled into his suite last night, after accidentally driving to the boarding house and realizing his mistake, he saw the refrigerator and a card table set up beside it. Water would have to be gathered from the bathroom, but that was okay. At least he wouldn't have to dive into the huge refrigerator in the kitchen downstairs a couple of times a day.

Maddy was sleeping a foot away on the other pillow, and he discovered Guppy clinging to the footboard.

"Morning," he said. "Why aren't you in your sleep cage, or on your tree?" He figured his pets were a little unhinged from the sudden move. It had happened so fast, and they were all upset that Mrs. Potts had been taken away in an ambulance.

"Don't worry, everything will be okay," he reassured them. He got out of bed and headed to the bathroom, where he showered and brushed his teeth, then dressed.

"Who's ready for breakfast?" Jimmy called out. For once, Guppy didn't holler back. Jimmy was worried about their welfare. "This is not good."

He went into the living room and pulled out the bins of food from the new refrigerator, and opened the can of Maddy's wet food. He walked over to the fake tree, got the bowls and took them to the half bath and washed them. Jimmy looked around and grabbed a hand towel to dry the food bowl. There were no dishtowels available. He filled Guppy's water bowl with fresh water and set it in the holder in the tree.

He scooped out the parrot's favorite food into his bowl. "Guppy, breakfast!" When the bird didn't fly into the room, Jimmy returned to the bedroom, picked up the parrot and carried him to his fake tree. "Come on, Gup. It's time to eat." The bird stepped onto his tree and walked over to his bowls and began to eat.

Jimmy sighed in relief. He prepared Maddy's breakfast at the card table with a scoop of kibble and a half can of wet food, mixed together. "Maddy, come get breakfast."

She sprinted into the room when called, so that was something positive.

"Daddy's going downstairs to get his breakfast." He stroked Maddy's head and back, then ran his hands across Guppy's head. "Everything will be okay, Guppy. Just think of this as a vacation."

"Vay Cay!" Guppy belted out.

"That's it. We're on vacation! I'll be back soon."

JIMMY WANDERED down the staircase and headed to the kitchen, where he found Brian at the table slurping coffee and eating breakfast.

"Good morning," Duncan said. "Ready for breakfast? Annie, get Mr. Katz a cup of coffee."

"Jimmy, please. I don't think we've ever met," he said, with questioning eyes.

Duncan held out his hand. "Duncan Carver. I'm the cook. This is Annie Mays, my helper."

"Nice to meet you." Jimmy sat with Brian. "Morning."

"You look like I feel. Could hardly sleep after correcting all those lists," Brian said.

"Tell me about it. Guppy's freaked out. He slept on the footboard."

Annie delivered a cup of coffee and a glass of water to Jimmy, then returned with a plate of food similar to what Brian was tearing into.

"Thanks," Jimmy said. "When are we supposed to head back to the ballroom?"

Duncan piped up. "Mrs. Diaz left an hour ago. She told Jenkins to let you two sleep."

Jenkins popped into the kitchen. "Good morning. Did you sleep well?"

Both Brian and Jimmy shook their heads.

"Today will be better. Jimmy, I want you to show me what to do for your animals in case you aren't available," Jenkins said. "You need an emergency backup, and since Mrs. Potts is in the hospital, I'll take that position."

"Good idea," Brian said. "I should learn as well. Are you going to let them explore the house?"

"If I do, I'll need to set up a litter box downstairs for Maddy. And Guppy isn't always reliable to wait until he's on his tree before dropping a load on newspaper," Jimmy said. He finished eating, then emptied his coffee cup with one last gulp, and stood. "Ready for pet prep?"

Annie swooped in and cleared the table.

"Thanks for such a great breakfast," Jimmy said.

"Thanks again," Brian said.

He and Jenkins followed Jimmy out of the kitchen and up the stairs.

"Guppy, this is Jenkins. He's going to help take care of you and Maddy when I'm not here," Jimmy said. He led Jenkins over to the fake tree.

"Gosh, he's so beautiful," Jenkins said. "Can I pet him?"

"Yeah, he likes it when I rub him from his head down his back," Jimmy said.

"Hi, Guppy. I'm Jenkins." He stroked the bird.

Guppy squawked loudly, then said "Jenkins".

Jimmy showed how the bowls lifted out of the holders on the tree, then showed Jenkins and Brian the food containers in the refrigerator and more produce in the fruit and veggie bins. Jimmy had a moment.

"Oh, wow. I just realized that I'm going to be one of the people who depends on food delivery when I run out of Guppy's produce."

Then he showed them how to mix up Maddy's food, and where her litter box was, the bag of litter, and the scoop.

"Jenkins, do you have any spare dishtowels? I've had to use hand towels to dry the food bowls, and they don't get the job done efficiently," Jimmy said.

"I'll leave some on the bathroom counter for you," Jenkins said.

"We should get over to the ballroom," Brian said.

"I'm going to head over to the hospital first," Jimmy said.

"Tell Mrs. Potts I'll check in later," Brian said, as he took off down the stairs and out the door.

Jimmy and Jenkins walked down the stairs together.

"Thanks for helping with my animals, Jenkins. I really appreciate it. They were used to having the run of the house at Mrs. Potts' place. If you want to bring Guppy downstairs, hang a towel across your arm. He'll step off the tree and onto your arm, but you need to protect yourself from his talons."

JIMMY DISCOVERED Mrs. Potts had been transferred to a private room, which was a relief to know she was out of danger. He found her room, tapped on the open doorframe, and strolled up to the bed.

"Hi, Mrs. Potts. Wow, you look a hundred percent better today!"

"I feel like it also. What's happening today?" she asked.

He told her about his participation in the ballroom.

"I feel bad that I couldn't be there to help out. It's a massive undertaking," Mrs. Potts said.

"I was with Irma Sue Delaney's group, and she's got everything under control," Jimmy said. "Aunt Betty is like a drill sergeant. She left the house around seven this morning—I feel like a slacker."

"Is there any word about what was poisoned from the Foo?" Mrs. Potts asked.

"It must have been seasoning because there's a sign on the door that says if you bought anything from the spice and baking aisle, to bring it to the police station immediately," Jimmy said. "Have you seen today's special edition paper?"

"No, I haven't."

"Let me go hunt one down. There's several great articles, and Danny got some terrific pictures." Jimmy left the room and headed to the nurses' station, then backtracked downstairs when they told him they didn't have a newspaper. He found the gift store where he bought Mrs. Potts a newspaper and looked over the novels. He knew she liked both romance and mysteries, so he grabbed something he thought she'd like.

"Here you go. I hope you like this book. If not, donate it," Jimmy said. "I'm going to head over to the ballroom."

"Thanks, Jimmy. Hopefully, we'll be home before long."

CHAPTER FOURTEEN

WHEN JIMMY'S Honda CR-V pulled up to the ballroom, an 18-wheeler was backing up to the front doors that were stretched open. The big truck stopped and a swarm of people from the ballroom approached like worker ants. The door at the back of the truck was thrust open, then the ramp was pulled down.

Jimmy scooted around the people at the truck and ducked into the ballroom, which had been transformed since he left there last night. The place was looking more and more like the interior of a grocery store, with rows of shelving waiting for inventory.

He spotted his aunt and made his way over to her. "Hi, Aunt Betty. You should have pounded on my door this morning. What are we doing today?"

"Hi, Jimmy. Don't worry about it. I figured you'd be completely conked out, plus you have your animals to attend to," Betty said. "After the food delivery we're waiting to get from the four stores, things will get easier. I've opened an emergency account with a grocery supply company for all our needs. They'll deliver directly to us instead of us having to run all over the place."

"How'd you manage that?" he asked.

"When I explained to the CEO that I had more money than his organization did, and he ended his chest-bashing, we came to an agreement." She smiled slyly. "Money has its rewards, along with a high Dun and Bradstreet rating."

Jimmy took in the activity. People were wiping down the shelves. Others were hanging signs on each end of the shelves to identify the number and contents. He noticed where the refrigerated and frozen areas were and saw odd activity.

"What are they doing over there?" he asked.

"Connecting the generators so the food won't spoil if the power goes out," Betty said.

"Wow! This is amazing. You've thought of everything! When did you start this entire process?"

"There was a flood almost a decade ago, and the ballroom was just about the only dry spot in the county. We set this up as our emergency home base. Mrs. Potts was instrumental in many of the processes that we're going through this time. She wrote out everything that we needed to do and how to do it," Betty said. "That woman is very thorough."

"That's amazing. What should I do to help?"

"We have to set up the checkout stands. Go see Ralph over there," Betty said. She pointed to an area away from the doors. "Once our trucks return, we have to stock the shelves. That will take everyone who was here yesterday to get it done."

"This is like setting up a grocery store from scratch. Oh, I almost forgot! Mrs. Potts is in a regular room! I'm not sure when she will be released from the hospital," Jimmy said.

"Dr. Canada will contact me when she's released, and she'll come to the house until her place is unrestricted, then thoroughly cleaned," Betty said.

. . .

FOUR HOURS LATER, all the shelving was in place, dusted and labeled. The checkout stands were working and the cool area was ready for content.

Then the trucks arrived.

Jimmy had never seen so much food in his entire life. Boxes piled high and deep in the huge trucks. An army of people with hand trucks unloaded the contents. Half the people tended to the trucks that held the nonperishables, and the other half unloaded the frozen and refrigerated contents.

The rest of the human force in the ballroom was lying in wait to sort where the boxes belonged. Before long, a lot of yelling back and forth was heard.

"Canned veggies."

"Beans."

"Pasta."

"Juice."

Then the corresponding aisle numbers were hollered about. Jimmy knew everything that went on aisle fourteen by heart, so he directed where those boxes should be unloaded. People cut open boxes and stocked the shelves. It was a smooth operation.

Once the last truck was unloaded and all the boxes were cut down, they all stood back to see their handiwork.

"Sara June? Send out the email!" Betty blared out. "The store is now open."

It didn't take long before people arrived for groceries. Unfortunately, they only had around thirty grocery carts, so people had to wait to shop until the carts were unloaded at cars and volunteers returned them to the ballroom store.

Jimmy manned a cash register. Every register had a helper on hand to provide a price for something that wouldn't scan properly. Against the back wall were paper and plastic sacks. The sackers seemed to be thoughtful in their sacking. They didn't want anyone to go home with crushed eggs or squashed bread, or one sack too heavy for a senior citizen to carry into the house.

Betty had figured people could work in four-hour shifts. The next day was a long day, with shifts beginning at six in the morning and running until midnight. Two days later, the grocer supply company truck arrived, and that had to be unloaded in between shoppers coming and going.

Danny and Brian were busy taking pictures and interviewing people throughout the entire operation.

It was a well-oiled machine, with the county matriarch gently applying the whip. No one else had the money or power to pull off this gigantic effort. That was the problem with living out in the middle of nowhere, 385 miles from the nearest shopping mall. On the other hand, in the tight communities that made up Starlight County, people came together and ignored their differences to take care of what needed to be done.

OLD MAN DAUTRY was found dead at his kitchen table. It was common to see him eating a sandwich on his front porch at lunchtime, but Brenda Miller, his neighbor, hadn't seen him in two days, so she pounded on his door. She found the front door unlocked, opened it and yelled out to her neighbor, expecting the worst. Brenda wandered into the kitchen and found him face-planted into a bowl of egg salad.

It appeared that he was salting and tasting his food prior to making a sandwich. Bread slices were prepped with mayo, lettuce, and a slice of tomato on a cutting board, waiting for their last content. The salt shaker was knocked over with its contents scattered across the table.

At first it was thought that old man Dautry died of natural causes because there was no evidence of foaming at the mouth, but since it had been over two days since his demise and being discovered, tests were performed to discover he had been a victim of poisoning.

People contributed to a growing shrine outside of the yellow police crime scene tape attached to the front door of his house.

SYLVAN AND BILL TRANCE were in a closed-door meeting. The poisoning situation was worse than a pandemic. There was no miracle shot to cure what was ailing their community.

"It would be prudent to go to a five-day publication schedule until this murderer is caught and things return to normal," Bill said.

Sylvan nodded. "We're already running special editions, so we might as well take up the cause, like you said."

"Why don't we see if Gigi is ready to come back to work?" Bill asked.

"Good idea. I'll call her," Sylvan said.

Bill stood and left Sylvan's office.

The publisher picked up the phone receiver, looked at a typed list, then dialed a number. It went directly to voicemail. He dug into his file drawer and pulled out an old employment application, noting another phone number. He tried that number.

"Hello, Mrs. Thompson?" he asked. "Sylvan Stonerich

here. I tried to call Gigi, but the call went straight to voicemail and there wasn't an option to leave a message."

Oh, hello Sylvan. How nice of you to call.

"Do you think Gigi would want her job back?"

Oh, Sylvan. No, she can't even read the paper with all the stories about the poisonings without breaking down. She's very fragile.

"I'm so sorry to hear that. Is she in therapy? Sounds like she needs help," he said.

She was seeing a psychiatrist who wanted to commit her to the hospital for ten days, but she refused that idea, then quit going to her sessions. There's not much we can do since she is an adult.

"That's too bad. It's terrible she's going through this, and I know it must be difficult on you and your husband seeing your child suffer so," Sylvan said. "Maybe it would be best not to mention my call then."

They said their goodbyes, and he hung up. It was sad for him to think how the once vibrant woman had fallen apart after that boyfriend dumped her and moved out of town. He stood, left his office, and walked the few paces to Bill's office. He filled-in the managing editor. They decided to have Milly text the staff to come back to the office for a quick meeting.

When everyone had gathered in the conference room, Sylvan handed the meeting off to Bill.

"As you all know, the TIN has published more special editions since this poisoning business began than we have since Jimmy moved to town and brought chaos with him." Bill smiled. "We know you didn't bring it intentionally, Jimmy, but that business sure sold a lot of papers!"

Of course, Danny and Brian, along with Eddie Garcia, the TINs tech wizard, scoffed at Jimmy's expense. Gert and Ag, middle-aged sensible women, looked upon those men as young Neanderthals.

"We're going to go to a five days a week publishing schedule until things calm down. If, after things revert back to normal, there's enough news to print, we may keep to the schedule," Bill said.

Sylvan stood. "I had hoped to bring Gigi Thompson back on staff, but I spoke with her mother and she said Gigi can't even read the paper without breaking down."

Gert snorted and shook her head.

Sylvan noticed. "Gert, everyone is aware that you had issues with Gigi, but I would suggest you check all your skeletons tucked away in their closets before you open your mouth and say a snide comment about that poor girl."

Gert grumbled to herself. She noticed Milly, the receptionist, smirking in her direction.

"This discussion will stay within these walls. I do not want to hear any gossip or bad-mouthing about someone who is suffering. Understood?" Sylvan glared into the room and counted nods. "Take over, Bill."

Assignments were handed out, then staff returned to work.

TOOMBS HELPED MRS. POTTS into the town car at the hospital, then drove her to the mansion where they were met at the front door by Betty.

"I need my clothes!" Mrs. Potts wailed. "I can't thank you enough for putting me up, along with the boys, Maddy and Guppy, but this is ridiculous, not having access to my clothing!"

"Let me show you where you'll be staying. I'm going to call Chief Price and have him get a definitive answer from Agent

Wilson as to when you can have access to your place, or settle back into the boarding house," Betty said. "I know the Wellness Center is still closed, and who knows how long the Foo will be closed."

Betty showed Mrs. Potts to a nice bedroom on the ground floor. A robe lay across the foot of the queen bed. "I picked up a couple of changes of clothes for you. I hope they fit. If not, they're exchangeable."

"Thank you, Betty. I think I need a nap. No one can rest in a hospital!"

Betty went to her office and called Chief Price. "Kenton, we need answers from Agent Wilson. Bertha was discharged from the hospital and is staying here, but her clothes and all her belongings are at the boarding house. Can you get him on the phone and find out when her place, the Wellness Center, and the Foo can get on with business?"

CHIEF PRICE GRITTED HIS TEETH. If things kept up the way they had been going, more closures were on the horizon. He pulled up Agent Wilson's number and smacked it with his finger. Four rings later, the least charismatic person he had dealt with in a long time answered.

"Wilson."

"Agent Wilson, Kenton Price, chief of the Twinkle Police Department here. What is the status on the boarding house, Jiltson Clinic, and the Wellness Center?"

Chief Price listened and responded with uh-huhs. "What about the Dime Water Food store?" More uh-huhs and nodding. "Okay, I will contact those parties and let them know." He disconnected without a farewell. He called Betty back.

"Mrs. Potts and Bill Hill will have to contact Lone Star

Hazmat Removal. They can't enter their places until a hazmat team has scoured the place from top to bottom. It will be costly." He listened. "The Jiltson Clinic was clean, so they don't require anything. Unfortunately, the Foo will be out of commission for a while longer. The dogs found more than just what was on the spice and baking aisle, so that's a ticking time bomb. It's a good thing the ballroom store is up and running."

When they hung up, the chief called Trembo Jiltson with the good news, and Betty Googled the phone number for the hazmat place and got them on the phone. She talked to a Jean Simmons and couldn't get the picture of the Kiss lead singer out of her head. It was determined that this type of hazard was easier to deal with than a toxic chemical spill. She booked the cleanup for the boarding house and the Wellness Center, provided payment, and that was that. Next, she got Bill Hill on the phone.

"Bill? Betty Diaz. Lone Star Hazmat Removal will be at your store on Thursday, around ten in the morning, so you'll have to let them have access to the place. Do not set foot inside your shop. Unlock the door. Understand?" She listened. "Not to worry, I paid them from petty cash. You'd better not order any stock until you find out whatever they used to clean up your place with won't leave a toxic odor or substance on surfaces. They will most likely have printed instructions." She listened. "You're welcome. That's what the Katz-Diaz Foundation is all about. Helping those in the community out of a critical situation."

Betty decided to let Mrs. Potts nap before she told her the good news.

CHAPTER FIFTEEN

Jɪᴍᴍʏ, Danny and Brian watched the people in hazmat suits wipe down counters, cabinets, appliances, all containers on the counter, the kitchen table and chairs at the boarding house. One guy waved his hand in a *get out of here* action when he spied them looking through the exterior kitchen door and taking pictures with their phones.

Once the hazmat people were finished with surfaces, they brought out a Swiffer-like contraption and used it to disinfect, or whatever it was called, the floor. One guy sprayed a solution on the floor, and another guy used the Swiffer thing. Then they turned their actions to all the bathrooms in the house.

It was at that point when Brian gave it up. "Let's go get something to eat."

They headed over to Biggem Diner for lunch and got settled at a table. Beulah Mae lumbered over to their table. "What'll it be?"

They placed their orders. She winked at Jimmy, then headed to the kitchen where she hollered out the orders to Bert before sticking the order slips on the clips of the order wheel.

Moments later, Celebrity and Ramirez joined them, stealing two chairs from nearby tables.

"What have you two been up to?" Jimmy asked. He was just a tiny bit jealous of all the time Celebrity spent with Ramirez. The deputy was a good-looking man.

"Trying to keep the peace," Ramirez said.

"We had to break up a fight at the ballroom before things got out of control," Celebrity said.

"Who was fighting?" Danny asked.

"The Tamborine brothers were squaring off with Jose and Pablo Gonzalez over hot salsa, of all things," Ramirez said. "The ballroom store can only stock so much. People have to get used to the idea that unless they want to drive hundreds of miles to a supermarket, the ballroom store is what they get."

"Salsa? Really?" Brian asked. "I hope they had chips on hand."

"Believe it. The grocery supply truck won't be back until tomorrow, and several of the shelves are bare. People have to make do until the Foo opens again," Celebrity said.

Beulah Mae returned to the table when she noticed the additional people. "Whatcha want today?"

Celebrity ordered tuna salad on stone-ground wheat, and Ramirez ordered a ham and cheese on a roll.

Beulah hurried back to the back and put a rush on the cops' meals. Sometimes they were wrapped to go when a call came in and they had to run.

"The hazmat team is over at the boarding house," Jimmy said. "They're supposed to go to the Wellness Center after that."

"I wonder when Mrs. Potts can go back home?" Celebrity asked. "Does the place have to be wiped down after those people leave? You know, to get rid of whatever chemicals they used?"

"I don't know, but I'm sure they have instructions for these types of cleanups," Jimmy said. "This has been a crazy situation. Guppy slept on my footboard, and Maddy slept on the spare pillow on the bed. They're both nervous."

Ramirez' radio crackled a call from Stephanie, the dispatcher. "Get over to Olander's Ice House and assist. Man down. Ambulance called."

Ramirez and Celebrity stood. He motioned her down. "I'll go, bring my sandwich when it's ready."

"Okay. See you in a few."

Beulah Mae noticed Ramirez heading out the door. "Move up the cops' orders! They have to roll!"

Within a few minutes, Bert put two white paper bags on the counter. Beulah Mae grabbed them and headed over to the table and plunked them down in front of Celebrity.

They exchanged cash. Then Celebrity was out the door.

"Bring me my lunch," Danny said. He slapped a ten-dollar bill on the table and was out the door.

"Do you think it was a shooting? *Man down* could be anything," Brian said.

"I hope it isn't more poison. That could mean all the convenience stores and ice houses could be shut down next," Jimmy said.

"I'm just glad they have all the volunteers they need for the ballroom store," Brian said. "Running the cash register isn't as bad as the lists, but you still have all those codes and things going through your head. Give me a story to chase any day!"

"I just want a solid night's sleep," Jimmy said. "Aunt Betty opening the mansion and giving us a place to stay was great, but I can't wait to get back to the boarding house and my routine."

THE NEXT MORNING there was chaos at the TIN. Not only was there another poisoning to deal with, but it shut another business down. In addition to that, Sylvan got the heads-up that Norbert Rosas, the District Attorney of Starlight County, was gathering statements from the adult Henderson children.

Both Hunter and Jeremy had provided sworn statements to the police departments where they lived, so their previously recorded statements could not be refuted. Celebrity was en route to Joslin's residence in Dime Water, and Ramirez was headed to Lockton for Marylou. The Henderson girls, now grown women, were to be brought in to Twinkle for questioning by the Chief and the DA.

At one point, Celebrity snatched her handcuffs that were clipped to her belt when Joslin became belligerent and tried to slam the door in Celebrity's face. When the handcuffs came out, Joslin had a change of attitude and came willingly. She was placed in the back seat of the cruiser and Celebrity checked in with the chief to let him know the circumstances, and that she was on her way.

Ramirez, being the good-looking hunk of a cop that he was, had no problem with Marylou, the youngest Henderson. Evidently, she liked men in uniform and chatted him up from the back seat all the way back to Twinkle.

The chief and the DA decided to question the women at the DA's office at the courthouse since it was friendlier than an interrogation room at the police station. Stephanie doubled as the court reporter and sat quietly in a corner with her equipment. She had already identified everyone in attendance.

Joslin glared at her sister. "Don't you dare say a word!"

Chief Price stared the woman down. "Why would you say that to your sister? Your brothers have already given their statements to the police, and they have talked to Mr. Rosas, the district attorney." The chief nodded in the DA's direction.

"Our brothers had no business telling you anything without talking to us first. I would have told them to bury that family nightmare," Joslin spewed out.

"So, Joslin, do you mean to tell me you were okay with what happened to your mother and your brother?" Mr. Rosas asked.

Joslin sat tight-lipped.

Marylou glared at her sister. "Joslin can do or not say whatever, but it's time our father was strung up from the courthouse square. He killed our mother, and he ran down and killed our brother. If she doesn't have the nerve to tell you what happened, I will."

"You were only a baby when your mother died," Chief Price said.

"I may have been a baby, but I remember Daddy holding a gun to Mommy's head, then putting the gun on the table and shoving those herbs in her mouth and forcing her to drink water. She shook all over, then her head fell onto the table." Marylou sobbed.

Mr. Rosas gave her a moment, then jumped in. "What happened to your brother, Boller?"

Marylou wasn't quite in control of her emotions, but managed to speak. "He was riding his bike into town to go to the police station. Daddy wouldn't let anyone use the car—he kept the keys with him at all times. So, Boller rode his old bike down the road, and Daddy rammed the truck into the bike. He stopped to make sure Boller was dead, then called Dude and Ramsey. They had a big fight, but then Ramsey got on the police radio and called for an ambulance."

The DA looked over at Joslin. "Do you have anything to add to your sister's statement?"

Joslin practically melted upon hearing her little sister state what she tried to keep her mind off of all those years. Gone was the anger and insolence. She sobbed uncontrollably.

Chief Price grabbed a box of tissues on the table and plucked a couple and pressed them into Joslin's hand.

"Every day, multiple times a day, Daddy would threaten us to keep quiet, or we'd end up eating poison like our mother. I had nightmares for years that he stood beside my bed in the middle of the night holding jars of poisonous herbs."

The DA turned back to Marylou. "Were you with your father in the truck when he ran down Boller?"

Marylou nodded, sniveling. "Back then, Dude was the DA, and Ramsey was the police chief. They're Daddy's cousins, so there was no one we could tell even if we wanted to."

The DA nodded to Chief Price. "I think we have everything." He stood, turned to the Henderson women. "Thank you for coming in and providing this information. It was very brave of you."

The chief stood. "We'll take you home now, if there's nothing else?"

Joslin jumped out of her chair. "Will you arrest our father? He's vindictive. He'll come after us." She nodded to Marylou.

"He's not going to be free to do that," Chief Price said.

"But if you arrest him and he posts bail, he's going to be free..." Joslin said, wailing in fear.

Norbert Rosas patted her on the back. "He's not going to be able to post this bail, I can guarantee it. And as for his cousins, they're going to be in that same leaky boat."

"Try not to worry," Chief Price said.

Stephanie led the women out of the room.

Chief Price turned to the DA. "Is there sufficient probable cause, Norbert?"

"Have Billy Boyd Henderson, Dude Richards, and Ramsey

Kent picked up. I'll bet either Richards or Kent, maybe both, will roll over on Billy Boyd. When the grand jury hears the proceedings, they'll indict," the DA said.

FORMER TWINKLE DA AND POLICE CHIEF ARRESTED

PEOPLE'S READING skills came into light when the police department began receiving calls wanting to know if Kenton Price, the current police chief that everyone liked, had been arrested after the newspaper printed the heading in two-inch tall letters splashed across the front page.

Then, apology calls were placed after people saw the pictures and read the captions and the articles. They discovered that Dude Richards, the former DA, and Ramsey Kent, the former police chief, had been arrested on conspiracy to commit murder, official misconduct, tampering with evidence, obstruction of justice, and perjury.

Next was a picture of a scowling Billy Boyd Henderson, handcuffed, who was arrested for the murders of wife Susan and son Boller Henderson. A picture of seventeen-year-old Boller and a picture of Susan on her wedding day appeared in the paper.

Ag Diaz shot multiple photos of the defendants at the two arraignments. First up were Richards and Kent, then Billy Boyd Henderson. Danny shot video of the proceedings to capture everything that would be broken down into articles and pictures for the next TIN issue and the website.

The TIN staff worked diligently to create the next day's headline:

BAIL DENIED FOR BILLY BOYD HENDERSON

Articles that followed outlined that Kent's and Richard's bail was set to $250K each. The pictures that accompanied the article showed disbelief on Ramsey Kent's face, acceptance on Dude Richards' face, and pure hatred on Billy Boyd Henderson's face.

Agent Wilson questioned all parties and determined none were involved in the current poisoning, so the FBI and local law enforcement were back to square one. In the meantime, the Stardust Ballroom continued to be the grocery store supplying the entire county, which canceled out two special events.

CHAPTER SIXTEEN

BERTHA POTTS SUPERVISED JIMMY, Brian, and Irma Sue Delaney, all wearing masks and kitchen gloves, on the proper way to scrub down the kitchen and bathrooms at the boarding house. She wanted to make sure that whatever chemicals Lone Star Hazmat Removal used to disinfect her house were completely eradicated.

She schooled Jimmy in the correct way to clean the table and chairs. "You have to go beyond the table surface, Jimmy. You have to clean the edge and under the edge because sometimes fingers touch places they normally don't."

Then she got after Brian and Irma Sue about the kitchen chairs. "Remember to scrub under the seat because most of the time you grab the seat to get close to the table." She demonstrated on the chair she was scrubbing.

After the house was deemed non-hazardous, Irma Sue left. Jimmy and Brian cleaned out the kitchen refrigerator and hauled trash bags to the trash containers outside. Then they tossed items such as milk and leftovers from their own refrigerators.

"I'm going to take a shower, then I'll go get Guppy and Maddy," Jimmy said.

"Good idea," Brian said. "Are you going to see if Toombs will help haul everything? If so, I'll drive."

"Let me give him a call." Jimmy manned his cellphone. "Hey, Toombs. We've got the boarding house disinfected. Can you help me load up everything to bring over here?" He listened. "Okay, thanks. I'm getting cleaned up. Should be there in less than half an hour." He shot Brian a thumbs-up.

"After I clean up, I'll head over to the ballroom to replace our food," Mrs. Potts said.

GUPPY HOLLERED *HOME* when Jimmy set his travel cage on the floor in the living room. Maddy dove onto a sofa cushion and snuggled down. The animals had missed their home.

After Toombs and Brian unloaded the last batch of Jimmy's possessions into his apartment, the fake tree was assembled, papers were positioned under the tree, and Guppy returned to work on squirrel invaders.

"Thanks so much, Toombs. The mansion is great, but this is home for us," Jimmy said.

"Everyone understands, Jimmy. This is where you settled," Toombs said. He thumped the heir on the back, then left Jimmy to finish putting things back together again.

Brian clomped up the stairs and entered the apartment. "Need any help?"

Jimmy leaned in and whispered. "Can you get the tools from downstairs and reinstall the cameras?" He nodded to the bag that was on the desk.

"You bet. We definitely want those installed!"

An hour later, they hauled groceries from Mrs. Potts' car,

then helped her put things away until she shooed them out of the kitchen. When they all sat at the kitchen table eating supper that night, they had a moment where they looked at each other.

"I'm so grateful we're back home again," Mrs. Potts said.

"I'm grateful for your home cooking," Jimmy said. "It's not that I didn't like the food at the mansion, but that was like restaurant food. This is real home cooking."

"I hope we don't have to go through that again!" Brian stated.

THE NEXT MORNING, Sylvan arrived at the TIN first. He flipped on the light switches at the back door and watched the place light up. Only a few moments later, Milly arrived and headed for her command center up front. Then Bill came inside, carrying the morning papers from across the state and country.

Danny came through the back door and walked over to his desk. There was a bottle of ibuprofen on his desk that hadn't been there the night before. His brow crinkled as he stared at it.

Gert and Deuce plowed into the TIN, followed by Eddie. A few minutes later, Agatha, Brian, and Jimmy arrived. Everyone wandered into the conference room for their early morning meeting.

Danny asked each of them about the bottle of pills. After everyone denied having placed them on his desk, he raised the alarm.

"All nine of you said you didn't place this bottle on my desk. There's only ten of us in this office, and I didn't put it there," he stated as his eyes went around the table.

"Have you touched the bottle?" Sylvan asked.

Danny shook his head. "Nope."

"Bill, call the chief," Sylvan said.

Milly jumped up. "You think the poisoner was here inside the TIN?"

"If none of us left those pills on my desk, how did they get there?" Danny asked.

Everyone plowed out of the conference room and surrounded Danny's desk.

"That means someone has a key to the place," Deuce said.

"Or someone picked the lock," Jimmy said.

"Milly, get George and Jerry Potts over here to change the locks and to make everyone a new key," Sylvan said. "It may be time to add cameras and an alarm system."

Chief Price, Ramirez, Celebrity and CSI Lloyd stood at the front door, which was still locked. The chief rapped on the door.

"Sorry, this is our early morning meeting," she explained as she approached the closed door.

"Do not touch the door handle," CSI Lloyd said.

"Let's go round to the back door," Ramirez said.

He, Celebrity and the chief walked away, while CSI Lloyd went to work examining the closed door for signs of forced entry. Then he unloaded his tools and checked for fingerprints on the exterior front door handle. When he was finished, he walked around to the back door.

Lloyd studied the lock at the back door and noticed the scratch marks. He pulled out a powerful flashlight from his kit and inspected the locking mechanism. He figured that any prints were most likely destroyed since the entire staff entered through this door. He still went to work, lifting what prints he could from the handle, around the handle, on the inside edge where the latch was, then the inside handle and area as well. When he finished, he entered the TIN.

"Back door lock could have been picked," CSI Lloyd said. "Found suspicious marks." He walked to the front door and went to work on the interior handle and surrounding area. He opened the door and examined the locking mechanism.

Nearly everyone stood around Danny's desk, staring at the bottle as if it contained a bomb.

Chief Price asked the obvious question. "No one here brought this bottle of pills and left it on Danny's desk?" After all the denials sounded, he asked, "What about the cleaning people?"

"They don't come until tonight," Milly said. "I'll call them just in case they did happen to change their standing date." She pulled up the phone number and placed the call. "Mr. Wynne, by any chance, were your people at the TIN last night? No, I didn't think so. It's okay... not to worry."

She turned to the police. "No one from the cleaning company was here last night."

Chief Price nodded to CSI Lloyd. "Handle it." He turned to Sylvan and Bill. "Make a list of everyone current and in the past who would have a key to the doors. When someone leaves the company, do they turn in their key?"

Sylvan nodded. "We collect keys, laptops, and anything else they might have of the TIN's in their possession."

Milly popped up. "George and Jerry Potts will have a record of anyone they made keys for. They're on the way over here to change the locks."

"Ask them to bring records with them, that is, if they haven't left their place yet," the chief said.

Milly got busy on her phone.

"Everyone else, please just stand back so Lloyd can do his best to find prints," Chief Price said.

"Has anyone been to their desk yet?" Celebrity asked.

"Not really. It's our early meeting morning, so people came

in, dropped things on their desks, then we were all in the conference room," Bill said.

"Maybe we should bag up the coffee cups?" Celebrity suggested, as she looked to Chief Price for direction.

The chief took a deep breath as he thought of the scenario. "Yes. Don't anyone touch your coffee cups. Let's not take any chances."

Celebrity slipped out the back door and returned with a box of evidence bags and gloves. "Why don't you all stay in the conference room while we bag everything up? Are there any cups in there?"

The TIN staff were ushered into the conference room.

"No cups in here," Gert called out. She looked over at Sylvan. "Can someone run out for coffee?"

"You and Deuce go next door. Make sure you bring enough sugar, creamer, and stir sticks," Bill said.

The Chief, Celebrity and Ramirez gloved up and started bagging cups. For the most part, it was easy to identify whose desks they were at. Three cups were found and bagged at Milly's command center. Then they headed to the tiny kitchenette, where more than a dozen cups were on the shelf over the coffee maker, and several dirty cups stood in the sink.

"Lloyd, should we take silverware, creamer and sugar?" Ramirez called out.

CSI Lloyd stood staring at the scene. "Go ahead and bag everything, to be on the safe side. We don't know who we're dealing with or what they did."

Deuce held the door as he and Gert returned with coffee, supplies, and pastries. They filed into the conference room and deposited everything on the table.

"I got an assortment of donuts and pastries," Gert said.

"Regular coffee—breakfast blend," Deuce said. He grabbed a cup, added his creamer and sugar, and took a sip. He let out an enormous sigh, opened a box, and grabbed a bear claw pastry.

Danny stared into space.

His dad thumped him on the back. "It's okay, son. Have a cup of coffee and a donut."

"It's not okay, Dad! Someone left a pretty specific message FOR ME with that bottle of pills!"

"Danny, have you had words with anyone recently?" Ramirez asked.

The reporter shook his head. "I can't think of anyone I've even had a difference of opinion with."

"No girls you dumped, or they dumped you? Someone's boyfriend getting in your face?" Ramirez prodded.

"I'm not Deuce! I don't go around dating and dumping girls," Danny said, while glaring at Deuce for his stupid affairs.

The office Romeo's face turned a bright shade of red at the reference that almost got him fired.

"By any chance would you have a box we could use so the cups don't get broken?" Celebrity asked.

"I've got one," Bill said. He walked to his office and dumped the newspapers that contained big red circles onto his guest chair, then brought the box to Celebrity. "Here you go."

Chief Price returned to the conference room. "We need to be realistic about this. Danny could have been the intended target. There's a good chance that none of the cups are tainted with poison, but there's no way to determine that until the results come back."

Danny seemed to wither in his chair.

"In the meantime, why don't you work from home until we get the results from the lab?" Chief Price asked.

The front door opened, and the locksmiths entered. Bill hurried to the front.

"What's going on?" George asked.

"Did someone break in?" Jerry asked.

"Someone left a bottle of pills on Danny's desk," Bill said.

Jerry looked askance until it dawned on him what the problem could be. "Oh, no!"

Ramirez approached them. "Did you bring your records?"

"Yeah, this spreadsheet goes back eight years," George said as he handed over a sheet of paper. "How many keys do you need?"

Bill called out to Milly to come up front. "Other than employees and the cleaning crew, does anyone else require a key?"

"That should do it, but let us have two extra keys for my lockbox," Milly said.

"Thirteen keys," Jerry said.

"Make it fourteen," Bill said. "I know, stupid superstition." He returned to the conference room. "New keys will be available in a little while, then everyone can work from home."

CSI Lloyd approached George and Jerry. "I think the back door lock was picked. I want you to examine the front and back locks and tell me if you see any indications of keyless entry."

"Okay, we'll get to work on the doors," Jerry said. He took the front door, and George grabbed his kit and went to the back door.

George examined the outside back lock. He saw the scratches Lloyd mentioned, but he determined that someone had missed the keyhole. Maybe it was the person who accessed the TIN last night in the dark and couldn't see very well. He commenced changing the lock.

"Everyone's laptops are locked in your desks, right?" Sylvan asked.

The staff responded in the affirmative. All laptops were tucked away under lock and key.

"Grab your laptops. We'll meet at my house or via Zoom,"

Sylvan said. "Milly, switch the phones over so you can take calls from your place. Better call the post office and have the mail held so you can pick it up. Eddie, we'll discuss what to post on the website. For now, I don't want anything about these pills leaked to the public until we know what we're dealing with."

"Got it," Eddie said.

"I want to keep this incident contained," Chief Price said. "No whispering to your family, friends or anyone else."

"We'll have your new key available when we get to come back to the office," Bill hollered out as everyone was grabbing their laptops and heading toward the door.

A chorus of *okays* as people piled out of the TIN office.

Bill and Sylvan stared wide-eyed at each other.

"We should be able to publish as usual from home," Sylvan said. "Let's figure out what we want Eddie to post on the website. I'll call you when I get home."

Bill went into his office, looked around and determined what he would take with him. His newspapers and laptop were the only physical items he could think of. The scheduling and layout software was on his laptop. Everything else should be there as well. He sat in his chair and opened desk drawers, thinking through the contents he viewed. Bill was grateful that the printing facility was at a different location and that they were not affected by this emergency closing.

After he was satisfied that he didn't need anything else, he grabbed his briefcase and the newspapers and went into the big room. The front and back door locks had been changed. George and Jerry were busy making keys. Sylvan was tucked into his office with Chief Price. Ramirez and Celebrity weren't around.

Bill stuck his head into Sylvan's office. "I'm heading out. Call me when you get set up at home."

"Will do," Sylvan said. He turned back to the chief. "I don't see what's to gain by hitting the TIN with this."

"This entire poisoning fiasco doesn't seem to have any clear targets. The Feds aren't helping either. Agent Wilson won't share information," Chief Price said as he stood. "I'll let you know when I hear from ChemLabs."

CHAPTER SEVENTEEN

JIMMY WAS CUDDLED on the sofa with Maddy, and Guppy looked to be napping on his tree. Terrible thoughts zinged through Jimmy's head as he thought of that bottle of pills on Danny's desk. None of the poisoned victims were connected in any sense when he considered the circumstances. Even though he, Mrs. Potts, and Danny were victims, all three of those events were so different.

He was delving deep into these dark thoughts when a loud rap sounded on his door. Jimmy practically jumped off the sofa, disturbing a snoozing kitty. Guppy squawked loudly in an accusing tone, having been jerked awake.

Jimmy opened the door to discover Moses Diaz on his stoop.

"Where have you been? You've missed your lessons!" Moses said as he barreled into the apartment.

"COMPANY!" Guppy squawked.

Jimmy looked at his parrot. This was a new greeting. Typically, the bird would holler out *invaders* or cops.

"I've been trying to stay alive," Jimmy said. "I helped my

aunt set up the ballroom, then we had to move to the mansion when Mrs. Potts was poisoned."

"Jimmy, you're the heir! You have to be able to take down someone when you're under attack," Moses said.

"There's not much you can do to fight poison, unless you have a poison-sniffing dog like the Feds used at the Foo," Jimmy said.

"But there's a person behind the poisoning act," Moses said. "You could come face-to-face with him. Maybe even forgot your gun that day, then it would be up to your training in self-defense to save your butt."

Maddy jumped off the sofa and wove herself around Moses' feet.

"Oh, who's this little princess?" Moses asked, as he stooped to run his fingers down Maddy's back, which earned him a loud purr.

"That's Maddy, and this is Guppy," Jimmy said.

Moses walked over to the fake tree. "Hi Guppy." He ran his hands down Guppy's head and back. "Your feathers are beautiful." He turned back to Jimmy. "Want to have a practice session?"

"Let me gather my gear," Jimmy said. "I'll meet you there."

"Okay. Better to be at the top of your game instead of on the ground hurt, or dead," Moses said.

JIMMY FELT as if he were being flung around like a doll. The padding on the floor of the dojo didn't help one bit. About fifteen minutes into his session, the private door opened and Celebrity entered, wearing her white two-piece outfit that sported a black belt.

Moses took a break. "My star pupil! Jimmy, take a break and let Celebrity show you how it's done."

Jimmy limped to the sideline and settled into a hard chair.

Celebrity and Moses bowed to each other, then proceeded to stalk each other in a wide circle. Then, in almost a blur, Jimmy's girlfriend was flinging Moses onto the mats. That only lasted a second, as his mentor sprang to his feet and was in a fighting dance with his opponent. Arms, legs, feet, and hands were a blur as they whacked and struck with force, and the fighters' voices shouted out sounds. Then it was over. They bowed to each other.

Jimmy stared open-mouthed at the woman he thought was so sweet. He realized she was tough as a cop, but this was a side of her he had never seen.

Celebrity and Moses walked over to Jimmy.

"Celeb, I had no idea you practiced here," Jimmy said. He touched the black belt reverently.

"Moses and I have been working out together for years," she said.

"I feel like a Neanderthal," Jimmy said.

"Everyone starts out that way, but if you keep at it, you'll earn your belts," Celebrity said.

He nodded. "I'll try not to miss anymore lessons."

Moses waved him back to the floor. Jimmy stood and presented sad eyes to Celebrity, knowing full well he was going to be soaking in a bath of Epsom salt later.

BRIAN WAS SITTING in the gazebo drinking a beer and reading a sci-fi book by a Houston author when Danny opened the door and came inside. He flopped onto the bench and grabbed the book out of Brian's hands.

"Survivor of the Mutant Dawn?" Danny asked.

"Yeah, I'm almost finished. Book 2 is supposed to be coming out next year," Brian said.

"Can I borrow it when you're finished?" Danny asked.

"Buy your own copy. I don't lend out books anymore. People either never return them, or they destroy them," Brian said. "Besides, the author would appreciate the sale."

They heard Guppy talking up a storm, giving the squirrels his opinion as Jimmy approached the gazebo. Maddy hopped onto the bench from her basket, while Jimmy let Guppy step onto the fake tree.

"Hey, what's going on?" Jimmy asked.

"No one's trying to kill me today," Danny said. He was still stewing over the bottle on his desk at work.

"Shouldn't the chief have heard something from Chem-Labs by now?" Brian asked.

"They're probably swamped with everything that's going on," Jimmy said. He eased onto the bench.

"What's wrong? Did you slip and fall or something?" Danny asked.

"It's called Mosesitis," Jimmy said.

"Mose... Oh, I get it. You've been to the dojo," Brian said.

"Did you know that Celebrity was a black belt?" Jimmy asked them. "You should have seen her and Moses on the mats."

"Yeah, she's won a few police events in self-defense in Texas," Danny said.

"Has anyone heard from Sylvan or Bill about how we're going to proceed with things? I don't think they want to let the public know that the TIN's shut down right now," Jimmy said.

"They've been working with Eddie about what he can report on the website," Danny said.

Suddenly, their phones all dinged with an incoming

message at the same time. They discovered Sylvan was inviting them to a Zoom meeting, although it wasn't an invitation; it was a work meeting they were required to attend. They worked their phones, waited while their audio and video were set up, then saw their coworkers already in attendance.

"Let's get down to work," Bill said. They saw he was in his home office. "Brian, Danny, I want you two to interview all poisoning survivors and get stories. Jimmy, I want you to get over to the Wojkenski farm and find out what, if anything, they are doing to keep their produce safe."

He looked down to read his notes. "Gert, push circulation. If we're going to publish five days a week, we need subscribers. Ag, help Eddie with the website. Sylvan and I have talked to him about content, but there's a lot of it and he could use help. Deuce, you've got the entire county to cover. We'll be able to fill more pages with school sports, the bowling league, and all the rest of it."

"What about me?" Milly asked.

"You're going to have to field calls. Be very careful that you don't let it be known that the locks have been changed or any of the rest of it. When we find out what the lab has to say about everything, then we'll follow with a story. In the meantime, it's business as usual, except you can work dressed down when you're at home."

Bill glanced across his screen at everyone. "Just don't do a Zoom call in your robes, people. Make an effort to look professional."

Deuce squinted at the screen. "Where are you guys?" He was referring to Jimmy, Danny, and Brian.

"We're in Jimmy's gazebo," Danny said. He was overridden by Guppy screeching out INVADERS.

"Is that a parrot in there with you?" Milly asked.

158

"That's my Amazon parrot, Guppy," Jimmy said. He picked up Maddy. "And this is Maddy."

"Oh, she's so pretty. Look at those blue eyes," Gert said.

"COPS!" Guppy alerted everyone.

Celebrity knocked on the gazebo door. "Can I come in, or are you busy?"

Through Zoom, Bill piped up. "You all have your assignments. Let me know if anyone has any problems or questions." The Zoom meeting signed off.

"Come on in," Jimmy called out. "We had a work Zoom meeting, but it just ended."

"Have you heard anything from the lab?" Brian asked.

Celebrity shook her head as she sat on the bench beside Jimmy. "We're still waiting. The chief is pacing the floor, not knowing the results. But let's face it, even when we get the results, what can we do with that knowledge?"

"It's not like we can hunt down someone who is so crafty that they don't leave any clues behind. They definitely are gloved up, and maybe wearing a disguise," Danny said in a sour voice.

He was not getting over how he had been singled out at the office. He was to the point where he looked over his shoulder all the time, but all he saw were townspeople. It could be any of them. Someone he grew up with. It was unnerving.

"You do realize that your desk is in the middle of the room, so maybe it was just a coincidence, or convenient to leave the bottle there." Jimmy tried to distract Danny from his personal hell of thinking he was singled out by the elusive poisoner.

Danny, Brian, and Celebrity appeared thoughtful.

"I hadn't thought of that," Danny said.

"Me neither," Brian said.

"You're right. It could have been a coincidence," Celebrity admitted.

"COPS!" Guppy belted out.

Jimmy popped his head up and looked. Ramirez was heading across the lawn to the gazebo. "Your partner's here."

Ramirez opened the door and stepped inside. "Man, this is the nicest gazebo I've ever seen."

"Mrs. Potts' nephews built it," Jimmy said.

"What's up?" Celebrity asked.

"No emergencies, no poisons. I was heading over to Francesca's for lunch and figured I'd see if anyone wanted to join me."

Everyone stood up.

Jimmy and Brian's phones beeped with incoming messages.

How many for lunch? Mrs. Potts texted.

"Do any of you want lunch here? Mrs. Potts wants to know because she's fixing it," Brian said.

"I'm in," Ramirez said.

"Me too," Celebrity piped up.

"Count me in," Danny said.

Brian texted *total = 5* to Mrs. Potts.

"Maddy, time to go inside," Jimmy said.

His kitten hopped into the Gazebo express basket.

Jimmy placed Guppy's towel on his arm. "Come on, Guppy, we're going back to the house."

"POTS," he hollered.

Ramirez opened the door and everyone piled out.

"Man, that bird is loud," Ramirez said.

They tramped across the lawn to the kitchen door and headed inside.

"Jimmy, Brian, pull out the table and insert the leaf," Mrs. Potts instructed.

"Where's the spare leaf?" Brian asked.

"Behind the pantry door," she said.

"Danny, help Brian. I'm bringing my animals upstairs." Jimmy took off down the hall and up the stairs.

"Everyone wash up. No dirty hands at this table," Mrs. Potts said. She pointed Ramirez to the half-bath. Danny followed Brian to his apartment, and Celebrity ran up the stairs to Jimmy's place.

"Grab two chairs out of the dining room," Mrs. Potts signaled Brian and Danny as they returned to the kitchen.

Jimmy and Celebrity joined the others in the kitchen, and everyone settled at the table in front of a plate of tuna salad sandwiches on whole ground wheat bread with mayo, romaine lettuce and a slice of tomato from Wojkenski's vegetable farm. They also had a cup of chicken and rice soup, a pickle, and a pile of chips on the sandwich plate.

"There's more soup if you want seconds," Mrs. Potts said.

"This is wonderful, Mrs. Potts," Celebrity said. "It's so kind of you to provide lunch for this bunch."

"I enjoy cooking, and it's always nice to have my table filled," Mrs. Potts said.

Ramirez studied Mrs. Potts for a minute. "Mrs. Potts, I realize this isn't the best table topic, but what did you feel, or experience when you realized you were sick?"

Mrs. Potts stopped eating and thought about Ramirez' question. "I remember reading my novel, and I had a little sample of the stew broth. Then, suddenly, I felt funny. Pain flashed in my head, and my stomach gripped like I've never experienced before. It was a bizarre feeling, then I must have passed out."

"I've wondered what people experienced from this poisoning," Ramirez said.

"I'm one of the lucky ones who lived to talk about it," Mrs. Potts said.

BETTY WAS *HAVING words* with the grocery supply truck driver at the ballroom. He refused to back the truck up to a convenient spot by the front doors, and his attitude of talking down to the matriarch did him in. No one talked down to Elizabeth Katz-Diaz and got away with it.

She pulled her cellphone out of her pocket and pulled up the phone number for the president of the company. By the time she was finished with him, the errant driver's phone rang. His facial expression changed from belligerent to pleading. When he pocketed his phone, he walked over to Betty and apologized profusely. Then he got in his truck and positioned it so it could be unloaded by the Twinkle and Starlight County volunteers.

The army of people with hand trucks was like watching a well-rehearsed ballet. A team rolled their hand trucks up and down the ramp. The sound of the contents of the boxes hollering inside the ballroom kept the hand trucks in motion to their final destination among the shelves. In no time, the truck was emptied, and it went on its way.

Irma Sue stood beside Betty. "Bet he won't forget this comeuppance for a long time... if he retains his job."

"Evidently that driver has never heard of the term *the customer is always right,*" Betty said. "He didn't even do his part to unload the truck, which was okay because we had that under control. But still, it was his job."

"You going to report him again?" Irma Sue asked.

"No, I think he's got enough on his plate if he doesn't get fired when he returns to the warehouse," Betty said.

They walked into the ballroom and took in the action. Volunteers unloaded boxes onto the shelves, making sure that older products were brought to the front. Customers shopped in-between stockers. It all worked out.

"No word on when the Foo will reopen?" Irma Sue asked.

"Nothing yet. The labs are most likely inundated with testing so many products," Betty said.

CHAPTER EIGHTEEN

CHIEF PRICE, Sylvan Stonerich and Bill Trance were stumped when the report came back from ChemLabs. Not one item that was bagged from the TIN offices was contaminated. Both the publisher and the managing editor were happy to hear that they could open their doors again, but the psychological torment had taken its toll.

"Do not publish a story about this," Chief Price said. "We don't want people to worry about someone breaking into their homes or businesses and messing with their minds."

Sylvan paced in front of the chief's desk, then faced him and his business partner. "If anyone asks why we were closed, what should we say?"

Bill had an idea float across his brain. "I know. We could say there was a problem with the server, or the internet connection, so we decided to all work from home."

"That would work because no one has to physically show up to repair the problem. It's mostly all done online." Sylvan nodded. "Good idea, Bill."

"Had you previously told anyone about the closing?" the chief asked.

"No, you asked us not to, so we've kept it under wraps," Sylvan said.

"Whoever is doing this is changing tactics," Chief Price said. "I don't like it. It's unnerving, and wasting resources—having all those cups tested."

"Will we get those cups back, or should we buy more?" Bill asked.

"Everyone can keep an eye out for yard sales," Sylvan said. "Guess we should contact the troops and meet at the office."

They shook hands with the chief and left the police station.

WHILE EVERYONE WAS GATHERED in the conference room waiting for Bill and Sylvan to update them, Milly handed out a new key to all staff members.

"No one's tested the keys, so maybe everyone should do that before the meeting starts," Milly said.

They all headed to the back door, then several of the staff swung to the front door. Eddie opened the front door and went outside. He tried his key, but it didn't unlock the door. He tapped on the door to get the attention of anyone to open it. Gert opened the door for him.

"Didn't work?" Gert asked. She inserted her key into the open door and turned it. Her key worked.

Eddie stared at his key. "Let me try it again with the door open." The key refused to even wiggle in the locking mechanism.

Deuce's and Ag's keys didn't work either. Everyone else could unlock the doors.

Milly opened her lockbox and checked those keys. Only

one worked. She sent a text to the locksmiths, and they responded by saying they would replace the keys shortly.

The staff settled back into the conference room and were joined by Bill and Sylvan.

"Sylvan and I met with Chief Price. The report came back from ChemLabs, and nothing was contaminated," Bill said.

Danny sat upright and stared at his dad and Bill. "That bottle of pills wasn't poisoned?"

They shook their heads.

"Nothing was poisoned," Sylvan said. "We had a long talk with the chief about it, but there's not much to say. Someone's using the previous poisonings as a psychological weapon, it appears."

"Who could it be?" Jimmy asked. "There's got to be someone who has a grudge against the TIN."

"It could be anyone. We've been publishing for a long time, and not everyone's happy to see their name in print," Bill said.

"Should we make a list of anyone who could be disgruntled over the past five years?" Brian asked.

"Then what?" Sylvan asked. "We don't want a witch hunt on our hands."

"Look, people, there's no way to get to the bottom of this. Whoever is doing this uses gloves and protects their identity," Bill said. "If the Feds can't catch this person, how can we?"

After much grumbling, their work meeting began. Assignments were discussed. Verbal progress reports were given. Just before the meeting broke up, Bill suggested everyone hunt down coffee cups at yard sales.

Jimmy headed over to the library on Andrajules Street to pick up a book the library had borrowed from a branch across the state. He noticed the huge truck pulling into the driveway of The Wellness Center, so he skipped the library and parked in front of the store.

He tapped on the door, but Bill Hill must have been out back, so Jimmy walked around the building. Sure enough, Bill Hill was waving at the driver to back up, then stop. Jimmy snapped a photo with his phone.

"Hey, Bill," Jimmy greeted. "Is that your inventory?"

"Yeah. It took a while to get the place cleaned before I could place my order," Bill Hill said.

"Do you have help to unload and restock the shelves?" Jimmy asked.

"It's just me," the proprietor said, overwhelmed.

"Want help? A bunch of us stocked the ballroom shelves. It will save you a ton of time and you'll be able to open tomorrow," Jimmy said.

"Really? You'd do that for me?" Bill Hill's eyes watered.

Jimmy manned his phone. "Give me a minute. I'll get people over here."

Within ten minutes, Brian, Danny, Irma Sue, and a couple of her people showed up with hand trucks. Bill Hill had the hardest job. He had to direct people to which aisles to unload cartons at. Once the truck was empty, they all went inside and the shelving began. Boxes were carefully cut open and products displayed on the shelves. When the shelves were stocked, Jimmy took a group picture with Bill Hill in the middle, smiling widely with relief. He grabbed a bottle of Wellness In A Bottle and walked up to the cash register.

"It's on the house," Bill Hill said as he thumped Jimmy on the back.

"Nope. I want to be your first customer." Jimmy grinned as he handed over his credit card.

Bill Hill rang up the sale. "That feels good. I need a sign for the door to let people know I'm open."

"Go over to the party store," Irma Sue said. "They have signs and banners."

"Did you install cameras?" Danny asked.

"You bet," Bill said. "Some are visible, others are hidden away, so no one will suspect they're being monitored. This sure has taught me a lesson. While I don't want to think there's a bunch of killers or shoplifters in my store, I'm never taking a chance again."

Everyone walked to the front door. "Thanks again for all your help," Bill Hill called out as people got into their cars and drove away.

THE MORNING PAPER showed pictures of The Wellness Center being stocked. At the time the paper went to press, the front door didn't have the banner attached yet, so Eddie doctored one of the pictures with a huge OPEN sign. They hoped people would flock back to the store to shop.

At ten thirty, Celebrity was reading the newspaper at her desk when Stephanie, the dispatcher, took a 911 call from Ralph's Ice House. A twenty-year-old from Little Pancake was apprehended by Ralph Junior. The man was screaming into the phone that he had the poisoner! All available police were up and out the door, including the chief, within seconds of Stephanie's announcement.

The dispatcher tried to calm Ralph. "Try not to mess up fingerprints on the item. The police are on the way and should be there in approximately eight minutes."

Sirens screamed down the streets, heading out of Twinkle. Half the TIN staff followed, then were joined by the remaining staff except for Milly, who manned the front, and Gert, who was in charge of sales, circulation, and classified. Even Deuce was out the door, pulling up the rear.

Ralph's Ice House sported twinkle lights that automatically

lit at twilight, seven days a week. They never closed. Major holidays were a lot of fun with people dropping off plates of food for the staff who worked their shifts, while everyone else in the county attended family dinners. The large parking lot filled with police and newspaper vehicles.

Danny stood way back to get a picture of all the cop cars parked haphazardly. Chief Price, Ramirez and Celebrity barreled into the establishment, followed by Peterson, Dupont, Brian, Ag and Sylvan.

Ralph junior, Ricky and Ronnie, jokingly called the 3-Rs, stood in front of the checkout counter bursting with excitement.

Ag and Brian stayed out of the way, but snapped pictures.

The chief scanned the place with his eyes. "Where's the suspect?"

"We locked him in the bathroom!" Ralph junior said.

Ronnie held up a gallon-sized plastic bag that held a bottle of maple syrup. "This here's what he pulled out of his pants and was fixing to set on the shelf!" The bag swung from Ronnie's nerves.

Brian got a good picture.

"Don't worry, I used gloves, so we didn't mess up his fingerprints." Ricky held up yellow plastic kitchen/bathroom gloves.

Ag let Brian take the pictures while she captured video for the website.

"Good work, boys," the chief said. "Let's go get our suspect."

They all walked to the rear of the store where the huge restroom sign hung. Ralph junior turned the key that was in the lock, and the door opened. A young man who was trying to grow a scraggly beard, sprung up from the toilet seat. He was in a clear panic as Ramirez reached into the bathroom, grabbed the suspect by the arm, and dragged him out into the open.

Within a few minutes, he was restrained in handcuffs. Celebrity stood in front of the suspect and read him his rights. Ramirez patted him down and found his wallet.

"Allan Humberg," Ramirez read out loud. "Little Pancake resident, just turned twenty. What do you have to say for yourself?"

"I'm not the poisoner! I swear! I was going to lift some maple syrup, but after I stuffed it down my pants, I figured that probably wasn't a good idea because of that poisoner running around messing with stores, but they caught me trying to put the bottle back on the shelf. I swear there's nothing poisonous in that bottle!"

He talked so fast, nonstop, that it was hard to keep up.

Chief Price studied the man. "So, let me get this straight. You were in the process of stealing a bottle of maple syrup, but thought that was a bad idea, so you put the bottle back on the shelf?"

Allan nodded swiftly. "Yes! That's how it happened! They wouldn't let me explain! I didn't poison anything or anyone!" He looked like he was going to pass out.

"Ramirez, take him to the station," Chief Price said. He turned to Celebrity, Peterson, and Dupont. "That should do it." He looked at the store's employees. "Come to the police station as soon as possible so we can take your statements."

They nodded like back window dogs.

Chief Price walked back to the front of the store, followed by everyone else. He secured the evidence, went outside, and got an evidence bag out of the trunk of his cruiser. He deposited the gallon bag into the evidence bag and locked it in the trunk of the car. The chief walked over to Bill and Sylvan. "Pretty sure he's not the poisoner. Just a kid trying to steal a bottle of maple syrup and changed his mind."

"I think this is about as much excitement as I can take for one day," Sylvan said.

"You going to run that by ChemLabs?" Bill asked.

"You bet. Can't take any chances, no matter how innocent that kid seems," the chief said.

ALLAN EMPTIED his pockets onto the counter, where Ramirez diligently listed every item on the intake sheet. He counted out the pocket change, which totaled forty-three cents, and noted it on the sheet. There were three sticks of gum, keys on a ring, a filthy comb, and a wallet that contained a driver's license, insurance card (expired), a picture of his parents, a photo of a dog, and eight-dollar bills.

Allen's one phone call didn't go so good. Evidently, Mrs. Humberg almost broke the sound barrier screaming into the phone. He hung up, knowing if he didn't get killed in jail, he'd get it when his parents bailed him out—if they had the money.

Ramirez let him stew in an interrogation room while he waited for the chief to return. When Chief Price walked into the station, Ramirez approached him.

"You missed the opportunity to have your ears cleaned out."

The chief scrunched his forehead. "Whatever are you talking about?"

"The kid called home. You could probably hear his mother on the other side of the street."

The chief shook his head. "Let's go talk to our boy." They walked down the hall to the interrogation room. The chief opened the door and sat across from Allan while Ramirez started the recording equipment.

After recording the date, time, and people in attendance, the chief nailed Allan with a harsh look.

"Explain what happened."

Allan was a lot calmer and talked at a normal pace. "Mom made pancakes, and we ran out of syrup, so I ran up to the icehouse to get some."

"Did you have the money to make a purchase?" the chief asked.

"He had eight dollars in his wallet," Ramirez provided.

"So, why didn't you buy the syrup? Why attempt to steal it?" the chief asked.

"I was saving that money for gas," Allan said.

They talked for more than an hour with the chief and Ramirez asking the same questions in different ways, and getting the same answers. Ramirez locked Allan in a cell, and they returned to the front of the police station.

Just as the chief settled into his office, the front door opened, and a middle-aged couple walked inside. They approached the front desk where Sgt. Butch Gonzales stood.

"Do you have my boy here?" the woman asked in a rather loud voice.

"Who's your boy?" Sgt. Gonzales asked.

"Allan Humberg," the woman belted out.

Gonzales called out to Stephanie, the dispatcher. "Steph, is there someone named Allan Humberg here?"

Stephanie gritted her teeth. "Yes, he was just booked in. Hold on a minute while I get the chief."

She picked up the office phone and pressed a button. An office phone rang in the back of the room. "Chief? Someone's here to see the prisoner."

Chief Price approached the front desk. "Are you Allan Humberg's parents?"

"Yes," Mrs. Humberg said. Her husband remained quiet

beside her. "How much is it going to cost to get him out of here?"

"Mr. and Mrs. Humberg, it won't be that easy," Chief Price said. He led them back to his office, and they all settled into chairs.

A tap sounded on his door, announcing CSI Lloyd. "I lifted the prints on the bottle. Going to drop the bottle off at ChemLab."

The chief nodded to Lloyd, then returned his focus to the couple sitting in front of him. "Your son attempted to steal a bottle of maple syrup from Ralph's Ice House. He was caught pulling the bottle out of his pants and setting it on the shelf. Because of the circumstances, the store employees only saw that part, which made them think he was putting a bottle that contained poison on the shelf."

"WHAT?" Mrs. Humberg hollered. "Allan isn't the poison-er!" She looked at her silent husband, who sat cowed in his chair. It was obvious who wore the pants in their house. "What's going to happen?"

"Your son will have to stay in jail until the test results are in. The district attorney isn't going to even discuss bail until we know those results," Chief Price explained.

The Humberg's sat silently absorbing their son's troubles. Mrs. Humberg stood. A moment later, Mr. Humberg stood. "Can we see our boy?"

Chief Price thought through the situation. "Give us a minute, then you can visit with him." He stood, went to his door, and hollered for Ramirez.

"What's up, chief?"

"Bring Allan to the visitors' room," the chief said.

"Sure thing." Ramirez eyeballed the Humbergs, then he took off down the hallway. A few minutes later, he returned and approached the parents.

"If you'll follow me." He brought them over to the intake desk and handed them each a square basket for their belongings. "Please empty your pockets into the baskets. Ma'am, you will have to leave your purse. I will lock it in this locker along with your baskets, and you'll hold on to the key." He pointed to a short row of lockers behind him.

Mrs. Humberg's mouth dropped open. It was obvious she had never visited anyone in jail before. She and her husband emptied their pockets, and she handed her purse to Ramirez. He locked the items in the locker and handed her the key.

"Don't lose the key, or you won't be able to get your possessions out of the locker," he explained. Next, he pulled a ledger out of a drawer and turned it to face them. "Please fill in this information and sign here."

They both wrote their names, address, the date, time, relationship to the prisoner, and signed in the space beside their information.

"Come this way." Ramirez led them down the hallway, through the secured door, and to the visiting room. He unlocked the door and let them enter. "I'll return in fifteen minutes." He left the immediate area and sat at a desk that was not visible from the room, but had audio and video.

CHAPTER NINETEEN

ALLAN RUSHED OVER to his parents, clearly agitated. "I'm sorry, Ma! Pa! I wasn't thinking!"

Mrs. Humberg hauled off and bashed Allan in the head. He flung his hands up in the air to avoid another slap. She thumped the back of his head with her thumb and finger. "Do you even have a brain in there? Or when they were passing them out, did you think they said trains and said you didn't want any?"

They made their way over to the table and chairs. Allan collapsed into the hard chair, and his parents sat opposite him.

"You're going to be in jail a while, son," Mr. Humberg said, in a quiet voice.

"They think you poisoned that maple syrup, you numbskull! You could go to prison, Allan," Mrs. Humberg said.

"For a long time," the father said. "Pretty sure your picture's going to be in the paper."

"You've brought shame down on our family. Isn't it bad enough we have to live in Little Pancake? Now we're going to be shunned by even those folks," Allan's mother said. "Why didn't you pay for the maple syrup?"

Allan cast his eyes onto the table surface. He felt bad that his parents had to deal with his indiscretion while he sat in a cell. "I don't know. I needed gas money, and didn't want to spend what I had."

"Well, there's nothing to be done now," Mrs. Humberg said. "Have to use a public defender if you need an attorney. God knows we don't have the money for that."

Ramirez sent a text to the chief: *How long do they get for a visit?*

The chief texted back: *Give them another ten minutes.*

Ramirez felt sorry for Allan. The kid made a bad judgment call at the wrong time. If the circumstances were different—if there wasn't a poisoner running around Starlight County, Allan would be facing a simple shoplifting misdemeanor. But in these troubled times, there was no telling what the district attorney would hand down.

Junior Stonerich was the public defender, so at least he'd have a strong chance of getting a fair deal.

Ramirez watched the screen. The Humbergs stood. He walked down the hall to the room and unlocked the door. "Ready to go?"

"Nothing left to talk about." Mrs. Humberg appeared defeated.

"I'll be back for you shortly." Ramirez held out his hand in a stop position, letting Allan know he should stay back from the door.

Ramirez led the Humbergs down the hall, through the secured door to the intake station. Mrs. Humberg handed over her key, and Ramirez placed their possessions on the counter and had them sign the book to show they received their items. Then Ramirez returned to lead Allan back to his cell.

JIMMY, Danny, Brian, Celebrity, and Ramirez sat around the table at Biggem's Diner eating lunch. They had a lively conversation about the apprehension of Allan Humberg, then Ramirez told them how Allan's mother hauled off and smacked him alongside the head.

"Man, I feel sorry for him when he's released," Ramirez said.

"He's not the poisoner?" Brian asked.

Ramirez shook his head. "That kid is no more the poisoner than I am. He just wasn't thinking when he got the idea to steal the maple syrup, then figured he'd better not and got caught putting it back on the shelf."

"Yeah, Junior's going to represent him," Danny said.

"I hope they don't hang him out to dry," Jimmy said.

"Pretty sure the judge will be lenient," Celebrity said.

Jimmy took a huge bite of his sandwich. The table quieted as everyone got the same idea and resumed eating their food. He let his eyes wander over the filled tables of the lunch crowd, and he was surprised to notice Gigi Thompson sitting at a table by herself with her purse on her lap. She nervously looked around, then ever so carefully, she swapped the salt shaker on the table with one from her purse.

He couldn't believe what he saw. Jimmy elbowed Ramirez. "Gigi Thompson just swapped out the salt shaker on the table with one from her purse!"

Ramirez and Celebrity were on their feet. They rushed over to Gigi's table and confronted her.

"Put your hands on the table where we can see them," Ramirez said.

Celebrity nodded to the purse in Gigi's lap. "Carefully open your purse."

"What for?" Gigi asked belligerently.

Beulah Mae Greenhorn approached the table. "What's the problem here?"

"This woman swapped out the salt shakers," Celebrity said. "Could be the poisoner."

Beulah Mae reached for the salt shaker.

Ramirez intercepted her hand. "Don't touch that. You'll corrupt the evidence with your fingerprints."

Beulah Mae pulled her hand back as if it were in a fire ant mound.

Celebrity nudged Gigi. "Open your purse fully!"

Gigi's chin wobbled. She was caught, and there was no getting around it. She opened her purse. The Biggem salt shaker was in plain sight.

Jimmy, Brian and Danny were busy taking pictures of what was going down. The entire diner became quiet as the crisis played out.

"Jimmy? Can you come here?" Celebrity called out.

Jimmy rushed over to her. "What do you need?"

She removed her keys from her pocket. "Pop the trunk and bring Ramirez two evidence bags and a pair of gloves. Grab one large bag while you're at it."

"Sure thing." Jimmy was out the door in a flash. He returned with the bags and the gloves. He handed them to Ramirez.

"Should I remove the salt shaker from her purse, or just bag the whole purse?" he asked.

"Not sure. Call the chief," Celebrity said.

Ramirez got the chief on the phone and explained the situation. "Okay. We'll be there soon."

"He said to take a picture showing the salt shaker in the purse, then bag the salt shaker, then the purse." Ramirez pulled out his cell phone and snapped multiple pictures of the open purse.

He labeled the bags. One for the Biggem Diner salt shaker in Gigi's purse, one for the salt shaker that Gigi had placed on the table, and one for her purse. He put on the gloves, then carefully picked up what he expected was the tainted salt shaker from the table and placed it in the evidence bag. He bagged the salt shaker from her purse, then bagged the purse in the large bag.

"Mirandize her," Ramirez told Celebrity.

Celebrity rattled off the Miranda Rights to Gigi. "Do you understand your rights?"

Gigi harrumphed. "Yes!"

Celebrity and Ramirez grabbed Gigi by the upper arms and forced her to stand. Celebrity cuffed the woman and led her out of the diner, with Ramirez following with the evidence bags.

"I'll box up your lunches," Beulah Mae yelled out to their backs.

Jimmy, Danny, and Brian followed their police friends out the door to continue taking pictures. After the cop cars pulled away, they returned to the diner and flopped into their chairs. They stared at each other for a full minute, digesting what had just happened.

"Man, it's a good thing you saw that!" Danny said.

"I've no doubt that the salt is poisoned. It's not like Allan trying to *unsteal* the syrup," Brian said.

"Well, Gigi did sort of go off her rocker," Jimmy said. "But I figured she was okay when I saw her working at the ballroom."

"I wonder what's going to happen to her? I mean, she's unbalanced," Danny said. "Can they convict someone if they're crazy?"

"Why would she do this?" Jimmy was lost in thought when

Beulah Mae came over to the table and boxed up Celebrity and Ramirez' food.

"Which one of you saw her?" Beulah asked.

Jimmy raised his hand. "Me."

She hauled him out of his chair and bear-hugged him.

"Uh...mrhuh..." Jimmy patted her on the back, trying to get her to release him.

Beulah Mae let Jimmy go and wiped tears from her eyes. "You saved countless people, Jimmy. I owe you!"

His phone dinged a text from Celebrity: *You need to come to the station and give a statement.*

He texted her back: *Okay, be there ASAP.*

"I have to go give a statement." Jimmy shoved the last bit of his sandwich into his mouth, chewed, then slurped down iced tea.

"We'd better get to the TIN and get this story written," Brian said.

"Yeah, and get these pictures sorted," Danny said.

They pulled out wallets to pay for their food, but Beulah Mae waved her hand. "It's on the house today!"

Jimmy grabbed the boxed lunches then headed for the door.

THE HEADLINE of the Twinkle Independent News the following morning was larger than life.

KATZ-DIAZ HEIR CATCHES POISONER

MRS. POTTS, Brian, and Jimmy ate breakfast while she read the article.

"That headline isn't actually accurate," Jimmy said.

"Why not?" Brian asked.

"Well, they need the lab results to prove she's the actual poisoner," Jimmy said.

Mrs. Potts looked up. "She could be a copycat, or maybe she didn't poison anyone. Maybe the salt shaker didn't contain anything bad."

"All I know is that the entire squad went over to the Thompson's house. They hauled out a lot of boxes and bags of things," Brian said.

"Pretty sure we'll find out soon enough," Jimmy said.

CHIEF KENTON PRICE, detective Benito Ramirez, and officer Celebrity Masters conducted an interview with Gigi Thompson while Junior Stonerich sat beside his client. Ramirez manned the video and audio equipment.

Chief Price began by detailing the date, time, who was in the room, and the purpose of the interview.

"Let it be known that I will address the defendant Gigi Thompson as Gigi," Chief Price said. "Gigi, you were apprehended and arrested at the Biggem Diner by Detective Ramirez and Officer Masters when witness Jimmy Katz noticed you swapping the Biggem salt shaker for a salt shaker in your purse. Is that correct?"

Junior Stonerich leaned in and whispered in his client's ear.

"I refuse to answer on the grounds that I might incriminate myself," Gigi said.

"Gigi, we searched your bedroom at your parent's house

and confiscated a container of a white substance we suspect is cyanide, a glue gun, and instructions on how to replace the seals on retail products. We will have the lab results back soon on the white substance. Were these items purchased locally, or from the internet?"

Junior nudged her.

"I refuse to answer on the grounds that I might incriminate myself," Gigi said.

The chief's eyes stared first at Gigi, then at Junior. He wanted information, but saw that he wasn't going to get anything. He pushed on.

"Why did you choose those specific retail stores?"

Gigi looked at Junior. He shook his head.

"I refuse to answer on the grounds that I might incriminate myself," Gigi said.

"Gigi, tell me why you left a bottle of untainted ibuprofen on Danny Stonerich's desk at the TIN."

Gigi's lip curled into a snarl as she glared at Celebrity across the desk. She jumped to her feet. "I'm not answering any more of your questions."

Chief Price stared at Gigi. "We're done here. Celebrity, return Ms. Thompson to her cell."

Celebrity stood and approached Gigi. "Either come willingly, or in handcuffs."

Gigi kept her lips buttoned and allowed herself to be led out of the interview room to the cell.

Ramirez stopped the recording equipment.

The chief and Junior Stonerich stood.

"You're not helping anything, Junior," the chief said. "That is one disturbed young woman."

"Chief, it's my duty to represent my client in the best way possible. When the lab results come back, we will have a better action plan," Junior said. "In the meantime, my client is innocent, no matter what the evidence points to."

Junior grabbed his briefcase and left the room.

Celebrity passed Junior on her way back to the interview room. "What are we going to do now? We've gone through everything that was confiscated, and there's no list of places she deposited poisoned items. Should we search her bedroom again?"

"I'm going to pay her parents a visit. Let's see if that produces anything." Chief Price stood and left the room. He stopped at his office, grabbed his hat, then headed out of the police station.

As he drove over to the Thompson's house on Popular Street, he thought about the sad business with their daughter and only child. This was a conversation he wasn't looking forward to. He parked the car and climbed the three steps and knocked on the front door.

Mrs. Thompson answered the door, eyes red from crying. She stared at the chief for several moments before she found her voice. "Chief Price, is Gigi okay?"

"I'd like to talk to you and your husband, if that's possible," the chief said.

"Sure," Mrs. Thompson said as she opened the door and stepped back to let the chief inside, then led him to the living room. "Have a seat. I'll go get Harry."

Chief Price stood in the room, taking in the wall of bookcases. The Thompsons joined him, and they all sat.

"I know this is difficult for you, but it's been a nightmare for this community not knowing if there are any other poisoned products out there," Chief Price said. He explained the wasted questioning session with Gigi and Junior.

"We don't know what happened, or why Gigi did this." Mrs. Thompson sniveled as she tried to stop crying.

"If there was anything we could do to help you, we would!" Harry Thompson said. "It's obvious Gigi is in worse shape mentally than even her psychiatrist thought if she's guilty of poisoning people."

"When we searched her room, we didn't find a journal or a list of the places she left poisoned products," Chief Price said. "Do you know if she kept a diary or anything like that?"

Mrs. Thompson popped up from the sofa. "Yes! She was always writing in her book." She went to the bookcase and was about to pull a brown book from a shelf.

"Please don't touch that!" Chief Price said. "You don't want your fingerprints on that if it contains what I think it might."

Mrs. Thompson yanked her hand away from the bookcase. "Oh! I didn't think about that."

"I'll be right back," the chief said. He left the house, popped the trunk on his cruiser and pulled gloves and an evidence bag out of his kit, then returned to the house.

Chief Price donned the gloves then carefully slid the book off the shelf, keeping his fingers on the edges so as not to destroy fingerprints. He turned and went to the coffee table and set the book on the table, then carefully opened the book and glanced at the pages.

"By any chance, would you have a pencil with an eraser?" the chief asked the Thompsons.

"Sure." Harry Thompson left the room and returned with a new yellow pencil that hadn't been sharpened yet. He handed it over to the chief.

The chief used the eraser to turn the pages. About a dozen pages into the book was where the entries became odd. It was at the time of her breakup with Tad, the Lockton man she had been dating, who moved to Dallas without her. It became obvious that something was wrong with Gigi's thought process as the chief browsed through the contents.

Chief Price kept turning pages. Approximately thirty pages later, he discovered the beginning of the madness. She had taped receipts for purchases, printed screenshots of products, and pages and pages of information on how to do specific things in regard to the poison, handling of materials, and every manner of the whole subject. After that, he discovered the section where she outlined the places she left poisoned products, what they were, how many, and when.

As he scanned through the pages, the worst he found was the hardest to read. That was where he discovered she had noted who was poisoned, who died, and her unbalanced comments.

Mr. and Mrs. Thompson sobbed through it all.

As the chief turned to the next to the last page in the book with any notations, he discovered an entry about the Wham-A-Rama Discount Store. He pulled out his phone. "Ramirez! Get over to the Wham-A-Rama and get that place shut down. Call the Feds. I found Gigi's diary, but I don't know what product is contaminated."

He turned to the Thompsons. "Hopefully, this information will save lives. Thank you for your help. I have to run." He enclosed the book in the evidence bag, then left the house. With sirens wailing, the chief's cruiser was down Popular Street, screeching around the corner and heading to the discount store.

CHAPTER TWENTY

THE POISON SNIFFING dogs were at work at the discount store. They discovered several spice jars that had been tampered with. Jimmy texted the chief, bringing it to his attention that Gigi had worked at the ballroom during the list building exercise. While she wasn't there when the shelving was put in place, or stocked when the food deliveries occurred, it was decided to send the dogs to the ballroom to rule out any possibility of poisoning.

Agent Wilson joined the chief at the police station where they sat in the interview room and went through the book page by page, capturing fingerprints, reading entries, and taking pictures of each page.

"I'm sure we'll be studying this book for quite a few years. If they had something like this back in the '80s, it would have helped tremendously in building a profile of the Tylenol poisoner."

After the book officially became evidence, Chief Price and Agent Wilson interrogated Gigi with Junior Stonerich attending. When her eyes fell on the book, she broke down, then agreed to talk against her attorney's warnings.

It was all in the book.

Only her fingerprints were on the book, on the pages, and on the items she taped to the pages. The book in itself was her confession.

At one point Gigi snarled out, "No one wanted me! Not Tad, not Danny, Jimmy, or Eric. No one wanted me!"

That outbreak stumped all the men in the room. Agent Wilson and Chief Price tried to piece things together, but Gigi clammed up on that subject.

After the grueling five-hour interrogation that Agent Wilson, more than Chief Price, conducted, they called it a day. Back in his office again, Celebrity and Ramirez sat before the chief.

"Celebrity, I want you to hunt down that Lockton guy Gigi was dating. We need to know why he didn't ask her to move to Dallas with him. It seems that was the turning point in her life," Chief Price said.

"Ramirez, we have pictures of every page of the book that's in evidence. I want you to go through them and make sure we haven't missed something—we can't have another poisoning, or another place that's a potential hazard that we overlooked."

The chief nodded to Celebrity. "Help Ramirez when you're finished interviewing the Lockton man. You both need to scrutinize that book. Read every word. Make lists of the places Gigi documented, what was poisoned, if it was recovered, and people she targeted. Don't overlook anything."

CELEBRITY QUESTIONED the Hunters in Lockton and obtained Tad's contact information. Mr. and Mrs. Hunter hinted that Tad had been dating two girls at the same time. When she left there, the deputy drove back to the police station to place the call to Tad. After three rings, he answered the phone.

"Hallo? Who's this?"

"Tad Hunter? This is Officer Celebrity Masters with the Twinkle Police Department."

"Oh my God! Did something happen to my folks?"

"No, your parents gave me your contact information. I need to talk to you about your relationship with Gigi Thompson," Celebrity said.

There was quiet on the line. After a long pause, he spoke. "She's not pregnant or something, is she?"

Celebrity gritted her teeth. "Not as far as I'm aware. Tad, your parents seemed to think you were dating two girls at the same time. Was this the reason you didn't ask Gigi to move to Dallas with you? Did you ask the other girl to go with you instead?"

"Gigi started to get very needy, and I finally had to break up with her. Yeah, I dated someone else at the same time, but just for a month or two, then we just quit seeing each other."

"Did Gigi get needy before you told her you were moving to Dallas? I'm trying to see where that neediness came into play," Celebrity said.

"Hmm." Tad must have been thinking of the situation. "I think it was after I got the job offer."

"So, is it fair to say that she was nervous that after two years of being together that you were not inviting her to move to Dallas?"

"Well, when you put it that way, yeah, that's about right," Tad said. "What's this about, anyway?"

"That's all I needed to find out. Thanks for your time. We'll be in touch if we have any other questions," Celebrity said, then disconnected the call. She cursed under her breath and stewed for several moments before getting up and reporting to the chief.

THAT NIGHT, Jimmy and Celebrity met for dinner at the Bull Ride. Celebrity guzzled her margarita while Jimmy had a beer. He knew there was something bothering her and wasn't sure how to go about broaching the subject when she jumped into it.

"I feel so sorry for Gigi," Celebrity started. "I had the most distasteful conversation with that piece of work she dated for two years."

"Can you talk about it?" Jimmy asked.

"As long as you don't write an article. This is strictly off the record, between me and you."

"I promise!" he said.

"She must have really loved the guy, but he wasn't in love with her. He actually dated someone else for a couple of months before he moved, while he was still with Gigi—keeping his options open, I guess." Celebrity bristled with anger the more she thought about it. "He had the nerve to ask me if she was pregnant. Like he'd take any responsibility for that!"

Jimmy shook his head. "Some people are not worthy of being in relationships."

"When he told me she was needy, I asked him if she acted like that before or after he told her he got the job offer in Dallas. He said it was after. What did he expect? She invested two years into that relationship and he didn't want her to go with him!"

"So that was when she started acting off," Jimmy said.

"You noticed that?" Celebrity asked.

Jimmy told her about the time Gigi hit on all the single men at the paper.

Celebrity stared at him for a long moment. "Do you know when exactly that was? Could help me in building the timeline."

Jimmy looked down at his phone and pulled up the record of calls. He found when Danny called not long after he started working at the TIN, when Gigi showed up at the gazebo. He held the phone up to Celebrity. "I'm pretty sure this is the date. You can check with Danny and Eddie as well. Eddie's girlfriend was there when Gigi showed up at his apartment."

"Oh, I bet that was an interesting conversation." Celebrity finished her margarita and contemplated ordering another, but decided she'd better not.

"Hopefully, now that she's in jail, there won't be any more people dying from poison she planted all over," Jimmy said.

"We hope not. There's still a chance that we don't know if all the places were discovered," Celebrity said. She shook her head in dismay.

Jimmy reached across the table and took her hand in his. "You know I'm not like that, right?"

"Oh, Jimmy. I'd never put you in that basket. You're not that kind of man. I'm pretty sure if you decided we weren't dating material, you wouldn't string me along. You'd most likely sever the relationship in a gentle way," Celebrity said.

"As long as you realize that," Jimmy said as he squeezed her fingers.

THE NEXT DAY, the Thompsons went to the jail to visit their daughter. Mrs. Thompson broke down when she entered the visiting room and saw Gigi.

"Gigi..." that's all Mrs. Thompson managed to get out. She couldn't stop crying.

"I want you to know it's not your fault I turned out this way. You were good parents," Gigi said.

"Why did you do this?" Mr. Thompson asked. It agonized him to look at the woman across the table, knowing she killed people and caused so much grief.

Gigi shrugged. "I wanted to get even with some people. Guys who brushed me off."

"But, honey, you poisoned complete strangers. Businesses have been shut down. The entire county has been affected by your actions, not just a couple of guys who weren't interested in you." Mr. Thompson stared at his daughter in disbelief.

She shrugged again. "That's the way things went. I can't undo anything."

Mrs. Thompson pulled herself together. "We'll help you in any way we can. You're still our daughter... our only child."

"Mom, there's nothing you or Dad can do for me now. I'll go to prison for the rest of my life. That's the way it is," Gigi said. She stood. "I'll most likely see you in court."

Ramirez came down the hallway and unlocked the door. He nodded to the Thompsons. "I'll be right back to escort you through the door." He held Gigi's upper arm and escorted her back to her cell. After she was secured, he returned to her parents and escorted them through the locked door.

THE NEXT MORNING, Celebrity balanced a tray of food for the prisoner. She approached Gigi's cell and noticed that the woman wasn't awake. "Gigi, your breakfast tray is here."

The prisoner didn't acknowledge her presence. Celebrity hurried back through the locked door, tray in hand.

"Chief, I think something's wrong with Gigi. She didn't respond to me when I brought her breakfast."

Chief Price stood. "Did you go into the cell?"

"No, I wasn't sure what to do, so I thought I'd come get you," she said.

"Leave the tray here. Let's go." Chief Price led the way back through the locked door to the cell.

The chief unlocked the cell, and they entered. He reached out and tapped Gigi on the shoulder. "Gigi?"

She didn't respond.

Chief Price felt for a pulse. He straightened up. "She's dead!"

"She's dead?" Celebrity repeated, stunned. "But how?"

Chief Price pulled his phone out of his pocket. He called the medical examiner, then the DA, then Agent Wilson. Ramirez joined them at the cell.

"What happened?" Ramirez asked.

"Don't know. Check the monitoring equipment," Chief Price said.

Celebrity and Ramirez rushed to view the video. There was nothing to see. Gigi ate supper. Read a book, got into bed, then went to sleep. There was no sign of distress.

Danny, Brian, Sylvan, and Bill Trance rushed to the police station when they heard the medical examiner was called to the jail.

Jimmy arrived, dressed in his white self-defense outfit with the white belt. "What's going on?" He took in Celebrity's downcast face.

"What happened?" Sylvan asked.

Chief Price shrugged. "It looks like Gigi died in her sleep. We won't know until the autopsy results come in."

"She died last night?" Danny spluttered.

After the medical examiner removed the body and

everyone else left the police station, the chief, Ramirez and Celebrity huddled in his office.

"This is going to raise a lot of questions. When people die in jail, it's typically because someone killed them... another inmate or a jailer who turned bad," Chief Price said.

Celebrity balked. "This is a small town. If the Twinkle police force had a corrupt cop, people would know about it, and they wouldn't stand by and let that rotten cop continue to have the job."

"I agree with Celebrity," Ramirez said. "Big City dwellers have every right to think the way you suggest, chief, but I don't think that applies in Twinkle."

"It happened here forty years ago," Chief Price said.

Both Celebrity and Ramirez flinched at the reminder.

"I'm glad Gigi had one last visit with her parents," the chief said. "Speaking of which, I guess I'd better go and break the news to the Thompsons before they hear about it on the news or read it in the TIN."

The chief left the building and drove over to Popular Street. He pulled the cruiser into the driveway and turned the car off. He sat there for several minutes, gathering his thoughts. Finally, he opened the car door, approached the house, and knocked on the door.

Mrs. Thompson answered the door and invited the chief inside. Mr. Thompson joined them in the living room.

"Mr. and Mrs. Thompson, I'm sorry to have to deliver bad news. It appears that your daughter passed away in her sleep during the night," he said.

They were stunned, silent for a long moment, then Mrs. Thompson sputtered out, "How? I don't understand!"

"What happened?" Mr. Thompson finally came to his senses.

"Celebrity brought a breakfast tray to the cell this morning, and Gigi didn't respond to her when she called out to announce breakfast. She hadn't opened the cell; she was standing on the outside of the cell holding the tray. Celebrity came and got me, and we went to your daughter's cell. She was cold to the touch and didn't have a pulse," Chief Price said.

The Thompsons sobbed at the news.

"We checked the monitoring equipment. Gigi ate supper, read a book, then got under the covers and went to sleep. We can only surmise she died in her sleep of natural causes, but the medical examiner will tell us the cause of death."

Mr. Thompson drew his wife to him. "This is better than her spending the rest of her life in prison. I wish we had a better visit with her, but at least we got to see her before she died."

"Did your daughter have heart problems, allergies, or any other health issues that could be responsible for her death?" Chief Price asked.

"No, she was physically healthy; her mental instability..." Mrs. Thompson said after she gathered herself. "I blame Tad Hunter for all those problems."

The chief left the Thompsons and returned to the police station. He checked on the progress of the notebook project. Ramirez was scrutinizing the photographed pages. Celebrity used a ruler to go line by line so she wouldn't miss anything. The chief figured they were three-quarters of the way through the notebook. He silently prayed there were no more notations of people, places, or things that were in danger of poison.

CHAPTER TWENTY-ONE

DR. MAXWELL, the medical examiner, walked into the police station. Sgt. Gonzales waved him back to Chief Price's office. The chief stood when Maxwell knocked on the open door.

"Hey, chief." Dr. Maxwell handed Chief Price a sheet of paper. "Autopsy report on Gigi Thompson."

"Let me hear it," the chief said.

"She died of natural causes. It seems her heart just stopped at approximately three in the morning. Not a heart attack. Nothing. It's a mystery," Dr. Maxwell said.

The chief stared at the man in front of him. "Maybe she figured her life was over with, and she didn't want to hang around for a trial and the inevitable prison sentence."

"Some people DO die from a broken heart. It's been documented. I guess this is in a similar category where she decided it wasn't worth sticking around," Doc Maxwell said. He shook his head. "Guess the TIN will be all over this. I hope there's no more poisonings."

Chief Price finally sat after the medical examiner left his office. His phone rang. He listened. "That's good. We need to return to some sort of normalcy. Thanks for letting me know. I'll get things put in motion."

Jimmy and Betty walked into the chief's office. Chief Price looked at Betty.

"Good news. That was Agent Wilson. The Foo can reopen."

Betty pulled out her phone and called Brink Hellman, the manager of the Dime Water Foo. "Brink, the feds called Chief Price. You can get the place cleaned up by Lone Star Hazmat Removal, then open to the public." She listened for a minute. "Once the cleaning has been taken care of and you're officially open, we'll box up the remaining inventory at the ballroom and bring it your way."

She disconnected from the call. "That's a relief. People can get back to normal. My volunteers have really put in their time keeping the ballroom grocery store working. So, what did Dr. Maxwell have to say about Gigi?"

The chief passed along the news.

"Sounds like she willed herself to die." Jimmy shook his head sadly.

"Her poor parents. Having to deal with the fact that their daughter was a murderer, then dying in her sleep at the jail," Betty said.

"Is it okay if I write about what the medical examiner said?" Jimmy asked.

"I don't see why not. I know you'll be kind," the chief said. He explained what the medical examiner had told him.

MRS. POTTS UNFOLDED the newspaper as she walked to the front door of her boarding house.

POISONER GIGI THOMPSON DIES IN HER SLEEP AT THE JAIL

"Oh, Lord." She noticed Jimmy got the byline for the story. She read the article on the walkway to the porch, shaking her head at every other paragraph. "That poor, troubled girl."

She climbed the steps, went inside and walked to the kitchen, where she poured herself a cup of coffee and opened the paper. The next article caught her eye.

Dime Water Food to Reopen Soon

"Wish they focused on that instead of Gigi," she muttered to herself. "Guess we'll be closing down the ballroom store soon."

Brian entered the kitchen. "Hey, Mrs. Potts. Don't count on me for supper. I've got a date with Lena Morales."

"Oh, wonderful! Don't forget to ask pertinent questions. Steer the conversation," she suggested.

Jimmy came into the kitchen. He thumped Brian on the back. "Got another date with that girl?"

"Yup. Going to give it another chance."

"Celebrity and I are going to do something; dinner and either a movie or just go for a walk," Jimmy said.

"You two have a good time. I may actually go out to eat!" Mrs. Potts said.

The two men left. Mrs. Potts smiled. Her two favorite young men were the apples of her eyes and her most favorite boarders, ever. "My money's on you two settling down."

The End

The Detectives

Jimmy Katz, heir to the Katz-Diaz empire, never has a dull moment with his two conniving animals.

Guppy, an Amazon parrot, and Maddy, his cat, are a picture of innocence. They learn language skills while watching children's programs on TV.

The town experiences a rash of identity thefts, one ending in murder. The thieves emptied the bank accounts. Meaty, the Foo IT guy, is on the trail.

The secret cameras Jimmy installed catch his animals watching Boris the Russian's YouTube videos on identity theft. They stumble upon who the bad guy is, but Jimmy realizes Meaty will have to come to the same conclusion for the police to make an arrest.

Jimmy writes an article for the Twinkle Independent News (TIN) about how to stay safe on the internet. Then there's the incident at the Starlight Ballroom...

ABOUT THE AUTHOR

 Dawn Greenfield Ireland is an award-winning author of 22 novels, including 5 series (cozy mystery, sci fi/fantasy, billionaire shapeshifters, and dystopian), and a stand-alone sci-fi romantic adventure.

Most of her 7 nonfiction books have won awards, and she has adapted a few of her screenplays into book format. She also created over 50 themed notebooks.

Two of her screenplays were optioned, and she worked on a screenwriter-for-hire project. Dawn has a certificate from the Professional Program in Screenwriting from UCLA (2002), and ScreenwritingU.

Dawn writes full-time. She lives among dreams and fantasies with two cats and moving boxes. Her head is filled with stories. She doesn't suffer from writer's block.

Her business, Artistic Origins, has been around since 1995. Besides writing, she coaches writers, edits, formats, and publishes clients' books.

Her former day job as an award-winning technical writer played a major role in her fiction writing. She is detail-oriented, the organizational queen of the known universe, and never misses a deadline.

Let me know if you find any bloopers I've missed.

Need an editor? Book formatter? Your book adapted into a screenplay? I'm your gal. Check out all my awards on my website, then click the Artistic Origins tab for all my services.

Please take the time to leave a review! Reviews help authors so much.

Sign up for the newsletter and get the inside scoop ahead of everyone else.

http://degreenfield.com

- facebook.com/dawn.ireland.18
- x.com/dawnireland
- instagram.com/DawnGreenfieldIreland
- goodreads.com/dawnireland
- linkedin.com/dawnireland

www.ingramcontent.com/pod-product-compliance
Lightning Source LLC
Chambersburg PA
CBHW050837180626
46814CB00007B/2511